Aggie Lichen;
Pilp Collector

Debra J Edwards

PurpleRay Publishing

Published by PurpleRay Publishing

PurpleRay Publishing is the book imprint of
Debra J Edwards
PurpleRayPublishing@hotmail.co.uk
www.purpleraypublishing.co.uk

Contents © Debra J Edwards, 2005

First printed July 2005
Reprinted November 2005
Third Edition May 2006
Fourth Edition December 2008
Fifth Edition November 2011

A CIP Record for this book is available from the British
Cataloguing in Publication Data Office

ISBN 978-0-9550192-0-3

Cover © Tara Bush

Prepared and printed by
York Publishing Services Ltd
www.yps-publishing.co.uk

For Ray, Kelly and Katey.
Without whose love and support
this book would not have been published.

For Mum and Dad;
they would have been so proud.

And for believers everywhere ...

Chapter One

I quietly slid my body between the wall and the back of my bedroom door. If I was quiet and waited long enough they might think I'd already gone. Perhaps they'd forget about me. But deep down I knew. I had escaped it for too long now. It was bound to happen. Any minute now the kitchen door would swing open and those immortal words would be uttered. All my hopes and dreams of peace and quiet would rapidly fly out of the window like a dragonfly with an express message to deliver.

CRASH!

Another chunk flew out of the wall as the kitchen door hit it with force. I took another deep breath, crossing my fingers and my wings tightly. Not tonight, please, not tonight!

'Aggie!'

I tried desperately to make myself smaller, sucking in my stomach so that I could hardly be noticed.

'Aggie, I know you're in there!'

The footsteps closed in, growing nearer and nearer to the door with each and every second.

Not tonight, please! Not tonight.

The door was pulled open and in an instant my hiding place was revealed.

'It's not up for discussion,' said the mean fairy, looking down at me. 'You're to take your sister with you tonight. She needs to learn the ropes.'

'But Pa, it's not fair.' I said, and threw myself on the huge tree bed for added affect.

'I said it's not up for discussion, young fairy!' he said leaving the room, the door slamming behind him.

Just pigging marvellous, I thought, dragging Bugface around all night again. It was *so* not cool! I wrenched myself from the bed and made towards the door.

I mean how long did it take to learn the ropes? You turned on the detector, waited for the beep sound and followed it until you found the stupid pilp. A gnome could do it with one hand tied behind his head!

'Oh, Whatever!' I said, stomping through the hallway. 'Come on then, Bugface!'

Myrtle, or Bugface as I preferred to call her, was my *darling* little sister – a nine year old pain in the neck more like. Being the older sister by four years, it was my responsibility to take her out pilp collecting until she was fully qualified. As I looked at her with her wild red hair and her poor taste in colour co-ordination – she took after Ma – I wondered if she would ever pass the test. For a start, she needed to grow a bit more. At fifteen centimetres high she was a little too short and weedy for a pilp collector (we're known as tooth fairies by humans) and she was unable to carry the weight of a full pilp sack. I, on the other hand, took after Pa; tall and lanky with a mop of straight black hair that defied all efforts – and there had been many – to make it curl in any way. Mind you, a night out collecting with dear little Bugface was enough to make anyfairy's hair curl!

For me, collecting pilps was a chore, something I had to do, something I was told to do, but for Bugface it was an exciting game. She still had no idea of the dangers involved. I watched her, perhaps a little envious of her naivety, as she left the safety of Ma's kiss and cuddle and made her way towards the front door. She pushed past, eager to join Bessie and me out collecting. Her pilp sack dragged along the floor behind her.

'And make sure you brush your wings properly this time. I'm not scraping you off the floor again tonight,' I shouted after her.

'You don't have to keep on about it. It wasn't my fault,' she whinged back.

'How was I supposed to know the pilp donor was still awake?'

'Err, doh! What d'ya think the pilp detector's for?'

One previous nightsgritch – a night on which pilps were collected – Bugface had made the big mistake of flapstopping – literally meaning to stop flapping the wings – when faced with a pilp donor. It took all my strength to haul her and the pilps back home to Pilpsville. Ma and Pa still blame me for it, but then I seem to get blamed for most things where my younger sister is involved.

'Aggie, come on! She's here,' shouted Myrtle, disturbing my innermost thoughts yet again.

'Yeah, and she's sick of waiting for you ...again,' came the dulcet tones of my best friend, Bessie.

Blimey, why was everyone in such a hurry tonight?

'AGGIE!' Bessie shouted again, losing patience now by the sound of it. 'Come on or we'll go without you.'

'Okay, okay, keep your wings on! I just need to get my sack.' I finished lacing my red boots, grabbed the sack and headed towards the door. 'You know there's many a fairy who'd pay to be my best friend.'

'Yeah, right,' said Bessie, pulling the thick brown jacket she was wearing around her.

'Nice jacket,' I said sarcastically. 'What's this one made from, fake squiggle fur?'

'Oh, don't start. You know what my granma's like with her nittin.'

I sniggered wickedly, 'Sorry.'

She pulled the jacket in even closer, and turned the collar up.

'Anyway, I think it goes beautifully with my eyes,' she giggled, flicking her hair to one side.

'Yeah, if your eyes were orange!' I added.

Bessie took a playful swipe at my head. I ducked just in case.

'So – are we ready now?' I said.

She nodded and we headed towards the door.

'Oh, no,' said Bessie, who'd reached the door before me. 'Guess who's here?'

'Who?' I said, pushing past her to see for myself.

And there he was – Gilbert, Groaning Gilbert, straining to see what was going on from behind the front gate, his thick black glasses tilted at an awkward angle. Gilbert Trickle, nine years old and already a legend in his own lunchtime. Far and wide, the word had spread of the vast moaning and groaning that left his mouth at regular intervals. The dull colours he wore reflected his constant sombre mood perfectly. He had the trademark Trickle hair; straight and dark with a crown tuft that just wouldn't lay flat.

'What the hell's he doing here? He slows us down, you know he does. Isn't it enough having to tow Bugface around all night?'

Myrtle gave me one of her pathetic 'you've really hurt my feelings' looks.

'Sorry, but he has to come too. Mum said he's too depressing to have hanging around the house.' The familiar voice was followed by an all too familiar face.

Enter one fearless Fred, thirteen year old brother of Gilbert, part time trouble shooter and breaker of limbs. The last time he was out with us we were almost caught at the crossing exit and Bessie's right wing was left in tatters. It took her a week to recover from such a traumatic experience, although saying that, I think she quite enjoyed all the attention Fred paid her as he tried to make up for it.

'You've got a nerve turning up here after your last performance,' I said.

'Oh, come on Aggie,' said Fred, 'that was an accident. I didn't know the sun was rising.'

'Yeah, come on, Aggie, give him another chance,' Bessie pleaded, 'After all, I've forgiven him.' She turned and shyly gave Fred a wink. Yuk!

'Fine, can we just get going, please? We'll never collect anything if we hang around all night,' I said, handing out my goodbyes to Ma and Pa as I spoke.

'Be careful. Look after your sister,' called Ma, 'Watch for the sun ... hold on, what's he doing here? He's a flipping liability. Poor Bessie ...'

'It's all sorted, Mrs Lichen, honestly.' Bessie cut in, 'It won't happen again.' She grabbed Fred by the hand and flew down towards the crossing, dragging him behind her.

'I was just going to say ...' Ma continued.

'It's all okay now, Ma. We've really got to get going or our takings will be well down. See you in the morning! Come on, Bugface.'

Nightsgritches often started like that, a ragged assortment of friends and hangers-on going out collecting. Usually Bessie and I would collect together with Fred somewhere nearby, just like in school in actual fact. Being all in the same class, we kind of hung around together which made the whole having-to-go-to-school thing not as bad as it could have been.

'Hang on, where's the fire?' It was Albert. He flew down to join us. 'Sorry, I was working on something.'

He's always 'working on something' if you know what I mean! What he actually does when he's 'working on something' is anyfairy's guess.

We flew swiftly downwards towards the crossing and joined Bessie and Fred. Bugface trailed limply behind, choosing to fly and sulk, with Groaning Gilbert.

Looking down I could just make out the other lands that made up the world of Mirvellon. Immediately below us, of course, was Pilpsville, land of the tooth fairies. Ahead was Spercham where the screeching sprites lived deep in the ancient Sporacious Forest, where they were able to practise their blood curdling screams whenever they felt like it. We were separated from them by a thin, but impenetrable, barrier that had been created by the healers to keep them at bay.

'I wonder how long it will really last?' said Bessie.

'It's impenetrable, Bess! It's supposed to last forever – isn't it?'

We looked at each other and shuddered.

Albert flew along side of us. 'We'd best wait for Gilbert and Myrtle to catch up. We can perch on that tree.' He pointed to a tall blue shret tree which stood at least fifty metres high.

They were brilliant for climbing and finding your way if you were lost. Bessie and I climbed up a little higher and looked around to see where the two missing fairies were.

'Look at all that smoke, right over there, in the distance. Where's it coming from?' Bessie asked.

'That's not smoke, Bess,' Albert shouted up, 'That's smog from Grublin City.'

Bessie's grip on the branch tightened as she heard those words.

'But it looks nearer than before, are you sure?' she said nervously.

'Use your noculars if you don't believe me,' called Albert.

'You do it, Aggie.' She thrust the noculars in my hands and clung on to the branch again.

Albert was right. The smog was indeed coming from the dreaded place where the Grublins lived – a walled city that sat on, and in many places sank in, the River Grub, near to the Creaganic Hills, far to the north of Pilpsville. It was the fear of their existence, and that of the sprites, that kept our senses, all six of them, alert each nightsgritch.

'Aggie!' screeched Bessie, 'What's that coming towards us? Is it a Grublin?'

'Pigging hell, Bess, you've made me drop the noculars. It's only Gilbert and Bugface. Now let go of the nice branch slowly and let's join the others.'

We climbed down, Bessie more cautiously than before, and found the others on a side shoot preparing to take off.

'Right, let's go,' shouted Albert.

There was a massive flapping of wings as we tried to make up for lost time.

'There's the crossing. We'd best be quick,' said Fred.

Ahead we could see the dying rays of our two suns which activate the portal known to us as the crossing. It lies between the enormous spreading roots of the sacred oak tree, where the healers live high up in its extensive branches. It was busy now, with fairies gathered in droves, waiting for the suns to set. In that split second as they finally hid behind the Creaganic Hills, the great white light opened to allow just enough time for us to be sucked in and spat out into the world of humans. It was quite a strange experience really. Pa often described it in simple terms as the 'door to the other side,' which I suppose was an accurate description. What it failed to say – in simple terms – is that we had only a limited time to collect – until the sun rose on the 'other side'. If we missed that deadline a cruel fate awaited us – humans call it death. Strangely enough, so do we.

It was a fear we had to face every time we crossed over but we were pilp collectors and pilps had to be collected. Besides, the donors, bless their little rotten teeth, would be expecting us.

All fears of screeching Sprites, gruesome Grublins and possible death were pushed aside as the crossing opened. The nightsgritch lay ahead.

****

The air on 'the other side' was crisp and the night bright and clear. The human's sun had disappeared from the darkened sky and had been replaced by a silver slither of moon. Perfect for pilp collecting!

The gang split up to collect from the surrounding donor houses while Myrtle and I hung around the immediate area. This was usual for tooth fairies with apprentices, or in my case big sister with Bugface in tow! The houses towered high above us, the numerous window ledges protruded from the walls inviting yet another landing. I looked around and could tell from the dim lights at the windows that some pilp donors were still awake.

We circled around for a while, giving me the opportunity to tease Myrtle by flying away from her, although this only forced her to try and follow me even closer. Then a faint light began to appear on the pilp detector and the faintest hint of a buzz could be heard.

'Stay close, Bugface. Pilp alert! Bugface! Bugface!'

There was no sign of her, great! Came to see the maestro at work and promptly missed the show. Where the hell was she?

'Sorry, my wings got caught on that tree,' she mumbled as she brushed herself down.

'Never mind that, come here. Look at the light. See how it's getting brighter and the buzz is getting buzzier.'

Now where'd she gone?

'BUGFACE!'

'Aggie, I'm over here,' came a shout. 'Can I go in now?' Myrtle had preceded the detector and was scrambling onto the pilp donor's window ledge, her scrawny leg dangling over the edge as she climbed.

'Not yet, wait for the light to go ...' Too late, impatience had got the better of her. She slid through the gap where the window closed and pressed her nose up to the glass of the inside window. At that same moment the donor's light went off. Phew!

Now pilp collectors are quite adept at getting through the tiniest of cracks in any window pane, that's not the difficult part. No, the difficult part is collecting the pilp from under the donor's pillow, a skill that requires much experience and years of practise if one isn't to get caught. Looking at the pair of skinny little legs that were sticking out from under this donor's pillow, I think it was safe to say that Myrtle hadn't quite understood the concept.

'I said wait for its head to turn then quickly lift the pillow with the left hand and retrieve the pilp with your right.'

'You said lift with your right hand retrieve with your left,' came a muffled reply from beneath the pillow.

A quick tug on the flailing legs and out she popped forcing us both to land noisily on the fluffy ground covering. The pilp donor stirred. We held our breath ...the donor turned over.

'Right, now listen carefully. Lift the pillow, take the pilp and sprinkle the dust. You got that?'

She nodded and flew up onto the bed, stealthily making her way up to the pillow which she lifted with extreme caution. The pilp, wouldn't you believe, was nowhere to be seen.

'I thought it was supposed to be here,' she call-whispered. 'You said it would be here.'

I gave the pilp detector a shake, the light was still

on. There was definitely a pilp to be collected. Myrtle let go of the pillow crossly.

'It must be under the other part of the pillow. Fly round, fly round!' I whispered back.

She landed on top of the pillow and looked down.

'Great, so how am I supposed to get under there with that great big head in the way?'

Hmm, I could see her point. I had to get her under the pillow without disturbing the donor – too much. A gentle shove would do it.

'Climb down, I'll give you a boost.' I called to her.

'But won't we wake it up?'

'Trust me. Just put your hands underneath the pillow, I'll hold your legs.'

She scrambled under the pillow, hands grappling frantically. Her head popped out again. 'It's near the back.'

I gave her a hefty push.

She immediately disappeared again. This time, just her right foot was visible. I gave her a few seconds then pulled her out.

'What did you go and do that for? I almost had it!' She shouted.

'Err, slight correction there, sister dearest. I think you may well have definitely had it!'

A large pair of sleepy eyes blinked furiously at

her. The mouth dropped open in pure disbelief. The donor was wide awake! It started grabbing desperately at the covers.

'Now the important thing here is not to panic,' I said, perching on the window sill to watch her reactions. Well, she was supposed to be learning the ropes after all!

'What'll I do, Aggie?' cried Myrtle, trying to dodge the grasping hands.

'Think about your training. What were you *told* to do?' I put my hands behind my head and leant further against the window. Myrtle continued to flit and flutter aimlessly around the bed.

'Err, dunno – I think I fell asleep at that bit.'

'Oh, for goodness sake! – just head for the window. – go through the gap.'

She flew up sharply. The donor leapt out of bed and started to wander around the room, eyes never straying from its prey.

'Aaaaaaahhhhhhh.' It grabbed frantically at Myrtle, missing her wing tips by just a few centimetres. Time to put an end to it. I dug deeply in my pocket and took a handful of magic dust and blew it straight into the donor's face. It stopped and stared at me, grabbing at the air in a kind of slow motion.

'Aaaaassshhhoo.' Wiping its wet nose on a sleeve, it returned quietly to bed. It turned over and went to sleep, blissfully unaware of its encounter with a real life tooth fairy.

'Phew! Now let that be a lesson to you!' I said, glad to reach the other side of the window. My relief, however, was not shared by the ever excitable Bugface.

'Wow! That was brilliant. Did you see its face?' She flew up and down several times, mimicking the donor's expressions perfectly. 'Shall we move on to another one, Aggie? Shall we?'

So much for lesson learnt! 'I think a quiet fly-round first, don't you?'

And so we left the emptiness of the window ledge, still pilpless, and began a gentle fly-round, giving us both time to think and re-focus on the task at hand – pilp collecting!

Chapter Two

The fly-round did little to quench Myrtle's thirst for excitement.

'Can we go to the big house now, Aggie, please?' she begged. 'There's always pilps to be collected from there, can we?'

'Oh, all right but you'd better behave!' I said. It was a five minute flight away but was always worth the trip.

Before long it was right in front of us. We flew over the tiny backyard which, as always, was littered with toys, large and small, broken and unbroken.

'How many donors live here, Aggie?' asked Myrtle.

I thought for a moment. There were certainly a lot of windows and it was four storeys high. I had seen many donors before of all shapes and sizes but hadn't thought of them in terms of number.

'Loads, Myrtle. Which means loads and loads of pilps. It's what I call a pilp collectors paradise.'

On cue, the pilp detector started buzzing.

'Fourth floor, Myrtle, red striped curtains – and mind the spider webs.'

Myrtle made her way clumsily towards a window ledge on the fourth floor.

The red striped curtains had been drawn tightly allowing just a chink of light to flow through. We waited, quietly hovering just below the ledge, keeping well away from the spider webs that lurked beneath. Ugh! That was one of the more yucky sides to the job – falling, or more usually flying, into web traps.

As soon as the light went off I nudged Myrtle gently and pointed upwards towards the donor's window.

'Oh, right!' she whispered. 'I'll meet you up there.'

'Be careful,' I mouthed. It served as a reminder that the window ledges of this particular house were in pretty bad shape and crumbled at the slightest touch. Ma had gone to great lengths to remind us of this, often using graphic examples of one-legged fairies who hadn't listened to the advice they were given!

I gave Myrtle a few moments to check things out before joining her. She was sitting with her back pressed firmly against the window. She looked pretty pleased with herself.

'I've checked carefully and the donor's definitely asleep.'

She cheerfully made her way to the crack where the window opened but her smile was soon to be dislodged by an unwelcome visitor.

'I think you'll find I was here first.' The familiar voice of Gertie Cruet rang out loud and clear as she landed awkwardly on the ledge next to Myrtle. Her long, pointed face was red with anger, clashing terribly with the frizzy brown mop that she regarded as hair. She was collecting alone which was a little surprising as there was always a crony or two hanging on her every word. A more unpleasant fairy would have been hard to find – here she was, practising being unpleasant.

'Clear off Gertie, this isn't your patch!' I yelled.

'Wrong! I saw the light, heard the buzzer and here I am, first,' she spat.

As the only child of the pilp plant manager, she only came out on nightsgritches to keep up appearances – and, of course, to annoy other collectors like me. She was spoilt silly and had all the usual nasty spoilt brat attributes. Today she was using the stroppy/ arrogant/liar ones to good effect.

'Move off, Lichen. I found it first.'

'Like hell you did …'

'Why, I'm surprised you can even pick up a signal with that old contraption.'

She pointed at our home-made pilp detector. 'Now if you had a new Splendiferous® pilp detector like mine you'd …' She stopped suddenly and looked all around. Her wings twitched back and forth madly.

'I can sense it too,' I said, taking hold of Myrtle's hand and pulling her closer to me.

There was something out there … spying on us. A breeze caught the leaves on the trees nearby causing them to rustle eerily. A shiver ran down my back.

'What is it Aggie? What's out there?' muttered Myrtle.

I adjusted my wings to home in better. 'I can't make out what it is. It's giving off a strange vibration. I'm not even sure if it's a fairy ...'

Whoosh!

Suddenly, from out of nowhere, a bright flying object flashed between us and the window. I jumped back, just missing the end of the window ledge. Pieces of old crumbling concrete tumbled noisily to the ground – which was a very long way down.

'Who or what was that?' I spluttered, steadying myself before turning round for a further look. My nerves were shot to pieces.

'Y-Yeah, right. L-L-Like you don't know. I bet you set all this up ...' came Gertie's reply, but she was soon cut short by the sudden shrill sound of a screaming fairy.

'Aggie! I can't stop!'

'Now what?' I turned sharply only to discover that another part of the ledge had crumbled. Bugface had fallen off. She was ... flapstopping!

'Hang on. I'm coming.' Gertie Cruet would have to wait.

I dived down, gliding carefully between the tree branches, trying not to damage my own wings in the process. She was dropping so quickly, much quicker than I thought. I accelerated, pushing myself beyond her loudly screeching body. I grabbed her arm tightly as I passed. The force pulled us harder.

'AAAArrrrggghhh,' we screamed.

Then we hurtled groundwards in a sisterly fashion.

'For crying out loud, Bugface,' I gasped. 'Start flapping before we both hit the flipping ground!'

'I can't! I'm scared and I've hurt my wing,' she sobbed.

There was only one thing for it.

'GERTIE!' I yelled.

'What?'

'If you're not too busy.'

'Well actually I've got a pilp or two to collect from your – this patch.'

I couldn't believe she was still sitting there.

'GERTIE!' I screamed, as loudly as I could manage.

'Why didn't you say?' she called out.

Did I have to spell out everything to everyone? Hello! Falling fairy! Life or death situation here!

Gertie swooped down to Bugface, took hold of her damaged wing then heaved upwards. Between the two of us we managed to get back up to the window ledge where she had been sitting pretty not too long ago.

'Thanks, Gertie. She was nearly a goner,' I said, settling a sobbing Bugface down against the window.

'Yeah, whatever. Pilp collecting to do,' she replied snootily, and with that disappeared inside the open window without a second glance at either of us.

She emerged just as swiftly.

'So just how the hell did you do that?' she barked. 'Try to spook me out and then get your little sister to create a diversion so that you can harvest the pilp, huh?'

'What are you talking about? A diversion? You call falling at 100 miles an hour with a battered wing a diversion? What are you, nuts?'

'So where's the pilp? I looked in the usual place, under the pillow, no pilp! It was there before. It was on the scanner. I saw the light, I heard the beep, I don't see the pilp!'

'Oh blow the pilp! That thing came right at me,' I said. 'You sensed it too, didn't you? Remember? Something bright, like a light. It came from the window.'

'No, Aggie Lichen, all I'll remember is being taken for a fool by you and your bugfaced sister! It won't happen again, you mark my words! This is *so* not over.' She began flapping her wings, getting ready to fly off.

'You saw it too, Gertie. I know you did.' I grabbed her arm to try and make her listen.

She pulled away and scowled. 'Like I said Lichen, this is *so* not over.' And she was gone.

I turned to where poor Bugface was sitting, knees tucked tightly under her chin, head down.

'Hey, Bugface. Did you see anything before you fell? Just the ground I suppose, huh?'

Poor Myrtle. She was still sobbing and shaking. I'd have to ask her later, right now I needed to get her home, but how? I hadn't collected a single pilp yet and Ma and Pa were depending on me. No pilp, no credits to run the house. More importantly, no credits to buy a new dress for the annual pilpblast. If only I could find Albert …

And as if by magic, he appeared.

'Am I glad to see you, Albert! You must have a seventh sense.'

'No, I just heard Gertie Cruet cursing you very loudly as she flew past.'

'Well, Myrtle just had a very bad case of flapstopping – again. She needs to get home so that Ma can repair the damage to her wing. I can't go because I haven't actually collected any pilps yet and you seem to have … well, you seem to have rather a lot in your bag, Albert. A huge amount in fact!'

'I've only got a couple, Aggie, it just looks a lot. Besides I've got other bits and pieces in the bag too, not that it's any of your business!' he said.

'All right, keep your wings on! – And there was this strange whizzing light. It almost knocked me off the ledge. It came straight at me …'

Albert sighed deeply and took hold of Myrtle's hand, 'I'll see you at home.'

'But what about this light?' I tried again.

'I said I'll see you at home!' Then, with a look that could have cut through a pilp, he was off. A tearful Myrtle hung tightly onto his hand as he soared towards the crossing exit. It would be a while before she could fly solo or go on a nightsgritch. Oh no! That meant an extended training period, more nightsgritches with me! Oh, GREAT!

****

The rest of the nightsgritch passed somewhat more smoothly but I still felt a little freaked out by that strange menacing light. I was used to collecting on my own, but now I found myself constantly looking around, and the slightest noise set my wings on edge. Pilps were thin on the ground, or should I say thin under the pillow. Perhaps the detector was on the blink. Strange. Pa usually checked them before we left. At least the exit locator button worked. The light from the detector cast a long, white shadow straight ahead. Sun rise was approaching. At last it was time to head for the crossing exit and return to Mirvellon.

****

I was really late getting back and hadn't realised just how fine I'd cut it until I actually reached the exit. My mind kept wandering back to the evening's events. As I pushed the bar down on the exit door, still deep in thought, I was unaware of the sun winking at me as it began its long climb to the top of the world. At any other time I would have been through that door like a shot! Tonight, however, was different and I was distracted. Boy, did I pay for it! The suns rays caught the top part of my wing and burnt through it like hot butter.

'Youch! Can this night get any better?' I wondered aloud, thinking that the answer to that was a firm no!

With my wing throbbing painfully, I swooped low over the buildings of my home town of Incisorton, which glowed faintly in the full skylight. The other towns of Pilpsville were spread out in front of me. The grand three storey buildings of Great Molaring and Premolam, built out of pilp bricks, looked down on the smaller houses of Incisorton and Canningford. Their roofs, made from silver scrigger (known as 'fillings' by humans), glittered brightly and the enamel bricks gleamed. But they were no match for the Pilp Plant at the centre, which glistened brightest of all. As I flew by, I caught sight of my reflection in its vast mirrored windows. I could hear the suction of the sparkle extractor as it yielded the magic dust and the sound of the pilp crusher hard at work, grinding the pilps to produce energy.

Home at last. I drew a deep breath knowing that questions would be asked and answers would be expected – correct answers!

****

'So exactly how many pilps did you collect?' Ma enquired sarcastically. 'I need to exchange them for credits tomorrow.'

'Well, I'm not sure ... exactly,' I said.

'How am I going to buy more magic dust without credits?' she continued. 'No magic dust means the donors won't get a metal disc under their pillow ... then there'll be trouble!'

'Ma, it wasn't my fault. Like I explained, things didn't quite go to plan tonight. You see there was this light ...' I tried to reason with her but she was having none of it.

'No excuses, Aggie.'

'Ma, don't blame her. It was all my fault. I'm to blame,' blubbed Bugface. 'I've let everyone down.'

'But there was this light, Ma. It came straight at me ...' I tried desperately to explain.

'There, there, Myrtle. You're not to blame. You're just an apprentice. Aggie was supposed to be looking after you,' said Ma, moving forward to give the injured party a hug.

'What's all the fuss?' Albert walked in. He looked relaxed and somewhat smug! Probably all those pilps he had in his sack – not that I could see any of them anywhere.

'Albert, I was just trying to tell Ma about the whizzing light. You know, the one that came straight at me ...'

He leant his skinny torso casually against the door frame. His long fringe hung like curtains over his eyes which glared across the room at me. The obvious sign of disbelief appeared on his curled lips as he whispered, 'You don't need to make up excuses, Aggie.' Then he turned to Ma and said, 'Aggie, did all she could, Ma. Myrtle really does need more practice at flapstopping.'

'Perhaps you're right, Albert. She needs ...'

Ah ha! See it wasn't my fault. She needs ...

'...to go out more often with Aggie. More flapstopping practice.'

Ahhhh! I give up! I was condemned to lugging a small sister around forever. I'll be ninety and still have her in tow.

'Sorry,' Bugface whispered on her way to the bedroom.

I poked out my tongue at her. Stupid Bugface!

'Best get some sleep now too, Aggie. Another long day tomorrow,' said Ma.

Sleep! Yeah, right, like that's going to happen. Nightmares about scary lights that only I can see, nightmares about falling off window ledges, nightmares about flapstopping ...

Chapter Three

Morning came quickly, the golden suns were shining, and school beckoned. Bugface, who was in need of repair wing-wise, was deemed unable to attend by a worried Ma and Pa. I was deemed able and therefore 'had better get those boots on' or would be late.

I'd already kept Bessie waiting for quite a while by the time I finally made it down the hallway. She was leaning heavily against the wall with her arms crossed. Her long curly hair had been pulled into two plump plaits and tied with bright pink bows.

'Nice dress.' I pointed to the pink flowery outfit she was wearing. 'Your mother's work, I take it?' I said sympathetically.

'Yeah, and that's not all.' She produced a silver crash helmet from behind her back.

'What's that for?' I asked.

'Well, your mum spoke to my mum about the incident last nightsgritch and now she wants me to wear this every time we go out collecting!'

'The incident last nightsgritch? Oh you mean *the light*. Yeah, well that was really scary – it just came out of nowhere, right at me – *whoosh.*'

'I meant Myrtle's flapstopping incident, actually,' said Bessie.

'Didn't Ma mention the light?'

'Well, no – not really. Are you sure you saw

– 27 –

something? You didn't, you know, imagine it, like.'

'I saw it. I definitely saw it … just wait here a minute. I made a little sketch – I'll just get it.' I ran back to my bedroom to find the tatty scrap of paper I'd drawn on.

'Oh for crying out loud,' screamed Bessie behind me. 'Come on, Aggie, old Fettock will have a right go. You know what a misery guts he can be. If I get a detention because of you …'

I returned promptly, puffing frantically. 'There, now d'you believe me?' I shoved the scrap of paper in her hand.

'It's a blob, Aggie, just a blob.'

'Honest, Bess. It was a fast, bright whooshing light – and hot too.'

She flicked the plaits behind her shoulder and shrugged. 'If you say so. Now *please* can we go!'

Hell! Why wouldn't anyone believe me? I pushed the scrap of paper deep into my pocket.

The short flight to school seemed to take forever. Bessie, grumpy in pink, ranted on and on about being late for school and what Old Fettock, the Headmaster of both Pilpsville schools, would do.

'He scares the wings off me, Aggie,' she said. 'He'll keep me in and make me write out the "What to do if you meet a Grublin" rules.'

'Bess, the only rule you need to know if you meet a Grublin is "fly fast".'

At last we reached the row where the two molar

shaped buildings stood. The carved silver pillars of Pilpsville Major looked impressive from afar. Emblazoned across the vast expanse of enamel was the school motto 'Pilpus Victorius'. This was where Bessie, Fred and me all went to *refine* our pilp collecting skills.

To the side of the school, was Pilpsville Minor, a miniature version of the senior school, where Myrtle and Gilbert were still studying the basics. Unfortunately for me, Myrtle found these 'basic' lessons extremely boring and on more than one occasion had fallen asleep in class. This now meant that she had gaps in her pilp collecting education and the only way to fill those, Ma thought, was by going on more nightsgritches with me.

'Do you need to drop a note in about Myrtle?' said Bessie, nodding towards Pilpsville Minor.

'No, Ma's already sent a message in via dragonfly.'

We flew in low across the courtyard, past the statue of Ivan the Zealous, champion pilp collector. The empty playground was a clear indication that the school bell had gone. A greater indicator was the closed door.

'Oh no!' cried Bessie. 'Now we'll have to knock at the door and then Fettock will know all about it and I'll have to write out the "What to do when you meet a Grublin" ...'

I didn't wait to hear the rest. I flew quickly up to

where our classchamber was and could hear the register being taken. My name seemed to feature heavily.

'Lichen?' (First time of asking).

'Lichen??' (Second time of asking).

'LICHEN?? (Sick and tired of asking!).

'Yes, here, present,' I gasped, flying swiftly through the now open window, boots scraping the window ledge, wing catching on the handle.

'Lichen, how many times have you been told not to fly through the window? Use the door like everyone else,' said Miss Thrune, our class tutor. She turned and smiled at Bessie who was being like everyone else and using the door.

I looked around the light cavernous chamber which was lined from top to bottom with ledges carved out of the enamel. There were very few spaces free for us to perch on. I couldn't see anything up high, our preferred position. The only places available were on the lower ledges – right opposite Miss Thrune.

'Here, Bess,' I called. 'There's a place here, next to me.' The words bounced off the ceiling and echoed for all to hear. Miss Thrune looked at me and tutted.

Bessie sat down beside me and began to unpack her bag.

I watched her intently. 'Oh hell!'

'Now what?' she said through gritted teeth.

'I've forgotten all my stuff.'

'You're kidding, right? Homework's due in today. You did remember that didn't you?' she said.

I pulled out a scrap of paper from my pocket and tried desperately to smooth out the wrinkles.

'You can't hand that in, Aggie. She'll go mad.'

I looked at the scrap of paper again and turned it over in my hand. There on the back was my picture of the light. Bessie was right. I couldn't hand it in. It was all I had to go on at the moment.

'Can I copy yours at break, Bess? Only I really need to keep this sketch of the light, you know, the one I saw last nightsgritch.' I tried to catch her attention once more.

'Yeah, but you'll need to get it off Fred. He forgot to do it too!'

'Talking of Fred, where is he?' I whispered, conscious of Miss Thrune's listening skills. Probably in some sort of trouble knowing him ...

The room became suddenly quiet. A long dark shadow appeared at my left side. I looked up to find Miss Thrune hovering directly above me. Her face was flushed with anger. Her long pointed nose more pinched than ever. And as she spoke a high pitched whistle attached itself tightly to every other word.

'Now, Lichen! Mr Fettock will see you now!'

'Sorry? Mr Fettock? Me? Now?'

'Yes! You! Now!'

Oh hell. That didn't sound good.

- 31 -

I made my way nervously down the corridor and knocked gently on the door.

'Enter!'

Mr Fettock was seated behind his desk, his ample portions squashed into a chair less than half his size. The snail-shell buttons on his brown suit jacket were only just preventing his stomach exploding from within.

'You wanted to see me, sir? Only I know I was a little late and yes, I know I'm often late and I came through the window when I've been told a couple, well more than a couple, of times I suppose if you're counting ...'

'Do shut up, Lichen. Sit down, please. A little dragonfly tells me ...' he began.

Damn dragonflies. Hate dragonflies.

'...that last nightsgritch did not go well,' he continued.

He stood up and leant across the table. His head tilted in such a way that his bald patch picked up the light from the overhead bulb and reflected directly into my face.

'It wasn't my fault. My sister, Myrtle, had a problem flapstopping. She kept falling. I managed to catch her, with some help from Gertie Cruet, before she hit the ground. She just needs a little more training.' I blurted out the facts from the nightsgritch, 'and anyway, if that light hadn't ...'

'Ah ha, *the light!*' He straightened up and came from behind the desk.

The conversation suddenly began to sound rather familiar.

'Yes, *the light!*' I said.

'And what light might that have been?'

Just then, a small figure emerged from the shadows of the room. Limping slightly to the left, an injury caused when he was almost trapped by a falling pilp donor window. So this was where Fred had been.

'I told Mr Fettock about the light, Aggie. You need to explain. It could be extremely important.'

'Fred, how would you know? You weren't there,' I said.

'Myrtle told me what happened. I called in to see her this morning, to see how she was after last night.'

Bugface! I might have known.

'The light, Aggie, tell him about the light,' said Fred.

'I'm not really sure. It was so quick. Just a flash.'

'But where did it come from? Where did it go?' questioned Fettock. 'Think carefully, this could be of great importance to the community.'

'Yeah, think carefully, Aggie,' Fred joined in.

But what else did I really know? Bright light. Fast. Bright light. Fast.

'I'm sorry, I can't think of anything else.'

'Well, if you do remember something, I would be most interested,' Mr Fettock muttered as he leant towards me. 'You may go now.'

'Sorry?' I said.

'I said you may go now, Lichen.'

As I left the room I couldn't help wondering about Fred's involvement in all this. Why would Fred be interested in the light? What did he think it was?

But these thoughts were edged to the back of my mind as I now had to face something even worse, something more awful than a visit to Mr Fettock. Yes, I had to re-join the class in the exploratory chamber for pilpology. A subject so mind-numbingly boring, and made even more so by the uninspiring teachings of Miss Thrune. Today we had to dissect and pickle a pilp – again!

'Come along Lichen, take a pilp and get carving. Let's see what you can find out today!'

Bessie had already started and was carefully drawing and labelling each part. I took a pilp from the bucket and stood at the bench next to her. There were no ledges in this chamber, just enamel benches at which you stood and worked but the cavernous echo was the same.

'What did Fettock want?' she said. 'Did he make you write out the 'What to do when you meet ...'

I quickly interrupted – her Grublin phobia was getting out of control. 'No, he wanted to ask me about ...' I looked around and made sure no-one was listening in, '*the light.*'

'What light?' she asked innocently. She hadn't taken in a thing I'd said but I did at least now have her attention and quickly re-told what had happened.

'Are you sure it wasn't Grublins hiding in the trees, rustling the leaves? I've heard tales of how they dress up as fireflies at night. Buzz, Buzz, Buzz!' She dropped her extractor noisily to the ground. Miss Thrune tutted.

'Stop it, Bess,' I whispered. 'Not Grublins, right? This was too quick for a Grublin. With their physique it's amazing how they get into the air at all. No, this was a hot, whooshing, bright light ... something odd about it too, as if it was watching us.'

'Oohh, that's just too creepy,' she said, 'but what's Fettock's interest in it?'

'Well, I'm not too sure. Perhaps Fred will have some answers. Let's catch him at break.'

But before any break could be had we had one more lesson to endure – the daily testing of our sixth sense, also taken by Miss Thrune. The idea was to home in on where she was hiding without looking. The trouble was she wasn't very good at this subject either.

'Where am I now, Lichen?' She called from behind the box of wing patches.

'Behind the wing patch box!'

'And where am I now?' She called again.

Hopefully, just inside the gate of Grublin City ...

******

The rest of the day passed without major incident. Unless you count the run in with the 'little dragonfly,' Fred. We hadn't caught him at break but we knew he'd be in wing maintenance. It was compulsory for all and was possibly the second most boring lesson ever. I caught sight of him quite accidentally as Bessie was oiling my wings.

'Right, now I want you to take the tip carefully in your hands like so and massage the hazel oil in gently. Be sure to use an upwards then outwards motion not outwards then upwards.' Mrs Carple demonstrated said motion on a Canningford fairy, I wasn't sure of her name but she turned as red as my boots the moment Mrs Carple began massaging the oil into her wing. There was a great deal of sniggering from one corner of the room but my attention was diverted elsewhere.

'Ow! Careful Bessie! The tip is still quite sore.'

The sniggering had been replaced with talking and I recognised Fred's voice taking part in the conversation.

'Ouch! Hell, Bessie! Are you trying to hurt me on purpose?'

'Sorry, I didn't mean to. It's just that you turned

round so sharply,' said Bessie, pulling a face.

It was Fred's fault really, making me crane my head round. I couldn't believe it! Gertie Cruet, great!

'Bessie, I thought you and Fred had an understanding?' I said, knowing full well how she felt about Fred. She'd had a crush on Fred for ages. The only problem was that Fred failed to notice her in that way.

'W-W-Well! Y-Yes! I suppose so!' Bessie stumbled on her words, more than a little embarrassed.

'So why's he so friendly with Cruet then?' If anyfairy knew the answer to that it was Bessie. She knew more about Fred than he did himself!

Now Bessie craned *her* head to see what Fred was doing.

'He's only talking to her, Aggie,' said Bessie. 'It's not a crime.'

Not yet, no. Only talking, but what was he talking about?

The bell for the end of school abruptly halted any time for further conversation. Tooth fairy schools traditionally only have short sessions due to the toll night duties take.

'Are you coming, Bess?' I asked.

'No sorry, I've got to look after the Sherner twins, while their mother goes to the pilpminder.'

Even pilp collectors needed pilpminders (known as 'dentists' on the other side), only we don't put our pilps under pillows, after all, who'd collect them? We just take ours to the pilp plant just like human pilps. We do have something similar though – a wing clearer. When our old wings fall off, there are new ones underneath, we leave them on the bedroom window sill at night and they are collected by the wing clearer who leaves us a small gift – a pot of wing oil!

Well, with no Bessie to accompany me and no Myrtle to collect from school I had no choice but to make the flight home from school on my own. Still, a little quality 'self' time was probably just what I needed … wasn't it?

Chapter Four

Flying home from school usually took around fifteen minutes so Ma always knew when to expect me. Today I was expected a little later as she'd asked me to make a stop off at the pilp plant to check how many credits we had made this week. It shouldn't be too bad, I thought, even though I'd had a bad night, Albert seemed to do well. Hopefully there'd be enough extra to use for my dress to wear to the pilpblast. I'd seen a really cool one in the shop and had been paying off the credits week by week. It was purple and yellow and would look so excellent with my purple boots. I'd already exchanged twelve credits for it. Only thirteen more to go and it would be mine. If I had a good collection that night perhaps ...

'Lichen, you say. Just when did you bring them in?' the pilp plant manager asked snootily, his long pointed face peering down at the line of hastily scrawled figures in front of him.

Lichen, indeed. He knew perfectly well who I was. Mr Cruet always did this to make himself feel superior. He would pretend that he had no idea who you were because to him you were not important. In fact your very existence seemed to intrude into his world. The only thing that mattered to him was the easy ten per cent he made from each pilp exchange. No doubt he also knew about my run in with his darling daughter. I didn't suppose she'd have to pay off her dress.

'This morning, Mr Cruet. Albert brought them in himself. He had a big sack just full of pilps,' I said politely. Ma always insisted that we were polite to him, 'Important man is Mr Cruet. Holds the balance of our livelihood in his scales.' Her words rang in my ears.

What seemed like an age passed before old Cruet managed to stop smirking and give me an answer. He pulled himself up to his full height, puffed out his chest and said, 'Ah yes. Twelve credits. Do you want that in dust or kept here as credits?'

'I'm sorry? Twelve credits? Are you sure? Twelve credits? That can't be right. Albert had a large sack, full, up to the top, loads. Twelve credits?' A slight panic came over me. A slight panic indeed, it was a major panic with all the other words a thesaurus gives you to describe such a moment of hysteria. 'Mr Cruet, I don't mean to be rude but I think you may have made a mistake. Would you mind just checking for me, please?' I asked, trying not to sound too desperate.

'My calculations are correct, missy. My calculations are always correct. Now run along. I'm an important man, I have things to do,' he snarled patronisingly, his red face reddening even more.

Missy! Missy!! Rude words came to the forefront of my mouth and it was all I could do to stop them forming even ruder sentences, but that didn't stop me thinking them! I made a hasty exit, a little annoyed and embarrassed at the same time. Ma's not going to be happy about this, I thought. Twelve credits went nowhere in a family of five, what with food, clothes, fairy dust. There was nothing for it, I'd have to get off home and break the news. But there was just time for a quick peek at my fabulous purple dress. After all, I did have to pass the clothes shop on my way home, well I did if I went back a few streets, back past the school, near the library! Just a quick peek ... and perhaps just a quick trying on session.

****

Mrs Flinge had owned the clothes shop, the only one in Pilpsville, forever it seemed. There was once a Mr Flinge but he'd met with the evil sun on the other side and been burnt to a frizzle, or was it a frazzle? So that left Mrs Flinge – Widow Flinge. Luckily for her, Mr Flinge left behind a huge amount of credits with Mr Cruet at the pilp plant. He now 'looked after' her interests.

I was greeted at the shop door by Mrs Flinge herself. Very odd but I suppose I was a paying customer even if I was a week-by-week-paying customer! She looked a bit put out, awkward like, fidgety even.

'I-I-I wasn't expecting you today, Aggie. I was about to close up early,' she said, her voice rattling nervously.

'Oh, I just thought I'd come and have a teenie weenie peek at my dress, if that's all right?'

'No, it's not all right. Like I said, I'm closing early today.' She started to pull the door towards her, only my foot stopped it shutting completely. I could hear voices within.

'What's that noise, Mrs Flinge? Sounds like customers to me. You can't shut the shop with customers still inside. What's going on?' She looked sheepishly at me as I pushed past her to see.

'I-I-I didn't know you were coming in. I-I-It's not my fault,' she stammered as she followed me through to the back.

An unwelcome yet familiar cackle echoed across the room through the scores of dress racks that were packed into the small stockroom. Though muffled there was no disguising that grating voice. There, in front of the large, gilt mirror, stood Gertie Cruet, public enemy number one, surrounded by her cronies, Petunia and Violet Millet.

'Looks good, huh? Came from 'abroad'. Purple suits me so much, don't you think so?' She twirled around, holding the dress as she spun. 'Needs to be taken in, though, as it's a bit on the big side.'

I gawped, gobsmacked, unable to fully take in what was happening.

'I don't like the length, either. Mrs Flinge, you'll have to take it up, right?'

My dress, she had it on! My dress!

'Mrs Flinge let me have it cheap, seeing as someone had already tried it on – several times,' Gertie spat callously. 'I'll have to get it cleaned before I wear it to the pilpblast.'

'I-I-I'm sorry, Aggie', stuttered Mrs Flinge. 'It's just that Mr Cruet gave me the impression that you wouldn't be going to the pilpblast and advised me to sell the dress at the earliest opportunity. I'll refund your twelve credits, of course,' she added, like that would make things better.

I fought to hold back the tears that were welling up in my eyes and swallowed to keep the lump in my throat from rising. How could she? She knew all along it was mine.

Gertie twirled around in the dress once more for her friends to admire, all of them giggling on cue.

I had to get out, I couldn't breathe. Pushing back through the clothes racks over to the door, I could hear the spiteful cackle of laughter behind me as I stumbled in desperation to leave.

'I'm so sorry,' called Mrs Flinge, as I ran from the shop, tears now falling freely down my face.

I managed to throw myself round the corner of the library and once there, out of view, cried for all I was worth. I felt stupid and humiliated. I'd walked straight into it.

'How could she?' I shouted. Knowing she could have any dress she wanted wasn't enough for her, she had to have mine.

I'd told her it wasn't my fault. I'd told her it was that flipping light but she didn't listen – neither did anyone else.

It was some time before I finally emerged, red eyed and red faced, from the safety of the library shadows. The journey home offered little comfort. I was very late now, not that I cared. Ma would be worried, not that I cared. Gertie Cruet had my dress, boy did I care!

****

A familiar shape flew out to meet me as I approached the family den – Albert.

'Aggie, where the heck have you been? Ma's worried sick, what with Myrtle being out of sorts, and she's been waiting for the pilp credit tally.'

I held my head down to try and cover my tear stained cheeks but Albert quickly realised something was wrong and pulled my chin up.

'Aggie? Aggie, what's wrong? What's happened? Was it those Grublins? I've heard they've been seen near town. Is that it? Shall I round up a few friends?'

Grublins! I could handle them, I just couldn't handle this.

'It's nothing. I caught my wing again. It just bought tears to my eyes. That's all.' A brave face was required at this point. Albert couldn't begin to understand how I was feeling and anyhow, I didn't care to explain to him or anyone else even if I had to lie.

Ma was certainly anxious and examined my wing carefully as Albert explained the reason for my red eyes. Unfortunately none of this covered my reason for being late. I had to think of something fast. I was going to have to lie again.

'I had to help Bessie with the twins as they were playing her up, you know, flapstopping and that.' The pathetic lie left my lips with ease. Ma seemed happy enough with it.

'Come and sit down. Dinner's almost ready.' She led me by the arm to the kitchen table. 'And how did it go with Mr Cruet?'

Now I had to tell her about the credits.

'Twenty-four credits, Ma. I've got twelve here. Mr Cruet held on to the rest as I didn't know how much dust to get,' I reported. What's one more lie? She'd never know – would she? Why should everyone else be miserable just because I was?

'Twenty-four? Is that all? I felt sure there was more than that,' said Ma, a little surprised. If only she knew! She scratched her head, turned and disappeared out the back door.

'So what really happened, Aggie?' whispered

Bugface, putting herself down beside me.

'Only I saw Bessie pass the window with the twins over an hour ago and ...'

'Nothing happened. Mind your own business, Bugface!' I replied harshly.

'I just wanted to help.' She sounded hurt.

'You can help me by finding another sister to pester! Another sister to put up with you and your stupid flapstopping! Another sister to share your stupid room with you! Just leave me alone!'

I turned my head away from her and felt the tears flow. I'd lied and lost my dress. My dress, my beautiful dress. How on Mirvellon could she help? Stupid, stupid Bugface!

Albert's arrival at the table diverted any further attention away from me.

'Did you hear all those rumours about a light, Albert? It showed up last night. Some kind of flying glow worm ...' said Pa.

Albert shrugged his shoulders and carried on eating.

'Well, I heard that it'd startled a couple of fairies so badly that they'd dropped their pilp sacks and lost their entire night's collection,' said Ma, shutting the back door behind her.

'Ow!' A voice squealed from outside.

'Oh, sorry Bessie, I didn't see you there,' she re-opened the back door quickly. 'Did the pair of you manage to sort those twins out?'

'Huh?' said Bessie, scrunching her face up.

I'd forgotten she was calling round to go to the pilp bar. I grabbed her arm and pushed her back out the door.

'See you later, Ma,' I called, following Bessie out.

'In a bit of a hurry, aren't you? Mind you, it makes a change!' said Bessie sarcastically as we took off.

'It's just that I had to stay behind to catch up on the work I missed when I went to see Fettock. No big deal, I just didn't want Ma to know.' It tripped off my tongue so easily. I had become a compulsive liar.

'Well, we'd better get a move on. Fred will be waiting for us. Oh, I've got some exciting gossip!' Bessie's face lit up. 'Apparently a giant fluorescent bluebottle has been terrorising pilp collectors. It was seen last night where you normally collect.'

'Blimey, Bess. It's not a bluebottle it's *the light!* That's what I was telling you about earlier! Remember?' I said.

'Yeah, well this bluebottle, I mean, light, whizzes past collectors, scaring the wings off them. And it's really, really hot. Somefairy's had her wing tips burnt quite badly.'

Exciting as this *news* was, I couldn't help thinking about my dress, my beautiful dress. Gertie Cruet would pay heavily for it – one day.

As we passed Fred's house, Gilbert flew out and tagged along behind us. He had a face on him like a bag of truffnuts.

'What's up with him?' I asked.

'Oh, something happened after school. He reckons it really wasn't his fault this time,' she said offhandedly.

'So what was it that he didn't do?' I asked.

Gilbert flew inbetween us and screwed his face up, 'I didn't do anything.'

'Yeah, that's what you always say. Now push off so Bessie can tell me what really happened.'

He retreated back behind us, cursing and spitting.

'Gertie Cruet apparently accused Gilbert of setting a web trap near her house. She walked right into ...'

The name rang through my head, bounced off my ears and hit me straight in the mouth. The response of my eyes was somewhat different. They decided to well with tears involuntarily.

'... the web, spiders and all. She was furious ...' Bessie continued.

I nodded, being totally incapable at that moment of forming even a simple, coherent sentence.

'Poor Gilbert said he was just turning the corner when it happened. Well she put two and three together and made a mistake – according to Gilbert anyway,' she concluded.

With tears forced back, I slipped back into the conversation gently.

'So if Gilbert didn't do it …' I wondered aloud, not that I really cared as long as someone did it.

'I didn't do it. I really didn't. I wish I had but I didn't,' groaned Gilbert.

'Who did do it then?' Bessie finished my wonderings.

'What's it matter, Bess? She deserved it, I'm sure. You know how unkind she can be,' I said, bitterly.

'Yeah, you're right. There are more important things in life. So shut up whinging, Gilbert, or we'll hook you on the tree again!' Bessie shouted.

'I was just saying,' whined Gilbert.

'Let me hook him up, Bess. We'll leave him there and pick him up on the way home'.

'Well, Gilbert?' asked Bessie.

Silence filled the air again. Groaning Gilbert became Gilbert the Very Quiet. Peace ruled!

Chapter Five

We found Fred leaning against the wall of the juice bar as arranged. He seemed to blend in well with the awful multi-coloured bricks that the building was made from.

'I hate those bricks, they stink!' moaned Gilbert.

He was referring to the fact that each brick was covered in a strange, and often foul, smelling fruit juice.

'Oh, do shut up,' said Bessie, 'and stop sulking!'

In between the bricks were three huge red windows giving everything outside a rosy outlook from inside the bar. A gigantic glass roof protruded awkwardly from the walls. This was entirely necessary as all the fruits and vegetables used in Mrs Cheric's juices grew inside the juice bar. They grew at an alarming rate and hung precariously from the ceiling, creeping stealthily along the walls and floor. But this wasn't the only strange thing about the plants; just a little stranger was the way they spoke to you as you passed!

'Watch out, Bess!' shouted Fred suddenly, as a golden girgberry lunged at Bessie's ankle. 'Quick, Gilbert, get the secateurs off the wall.'

Gilbert smashed the glass in the emergency

box with his elbow and grabbed the cutters. The girgberry had already wrapped itself around Bessie's calf and was heading for her knee.

'There,' said Fred, snipping through the plants stem, 'just in time.'

The plant squealed and retreated. 'Juicy fruits, I have juicy fruits.' It murmured as it crawled away.

'You've got to watch that one,' said Mrs Cheric, helping Bessie to her feet. 'He can get a bit frisky at times. I think it's that pretty pink dress you're wearing.'

Bessie frowned.

Mrs Cheric ushered us all inside, 'Come on, in you go.'

In amongst the greenery, were places to sit although the actual positions of the seating areas changed daily according to the growth of the plants.

The tantalising smell of fruit juices filled the air. We breathed in. It was totally intoxicating.

'It's been an such an odd day, Aggie,' Mrs Cheric broke in, wrestling with a blender full of sporch and girgberries, 'Earlier on some strange looking fairy came in with these grey bottles and asked if I'd sell them for him. I soon sent him on his way! And then this afternoon, two fairies came in and starting talking about a light. Then more and more arrived. Well, I've not had a minute's peace since then and Mr Cheric, well he's no use at all. He just gets under my wings so I've sent him out the back to pickle some truffnuts,' she said breathlessly. 'I don't suppose you could give us a hand, Aggie?'

'Well, actually I came here to talk about the …'

'Free juice all night?' she added quickly.

I'd helped Mrs Cheric out at a couple of teengrowth and uncurling parties which were often held at the juice bar. Teengrowths were usually great fun but uncurling parties were always a nightmare because although you knew the day that a fairylet's wings would uncurl – they started to turn transparent – the exact time of uncurling was never certain.

'Okay, you're on – as long as it's not gruesome gorch!'

Mrs Cheric smiled then went off to rest her wings leaving me in charge.

'Okay, what will it be?' I called to Fred and Bessie. They were propping up the far end of the counter near to the seating area where Gilbert had been deposited. I could tell from his face that he was still seething.

'Oh, just give me something for Gilbert, Aggie,' Fred sighed.

Hmm, a purple pipkin surprise should liven him up. A large pinch of scurd, a dash of fickle cordial and a pint of purple pipkin juice. Then give it a quick shake – you never stirred pipkin juice because of the adverse effects – and pour it into a long glass.

'Is it ready yet, Aggie? I don't know how much more we can take,' called Bessie, raising her eyebrows.

I gave it a quick stir, poured it out and handed it over. I watched as he guzzled it down, still moaning and groaning inbetween mouthfuls.

'So what have I missed, Fred. What news of the light?' I asked eagerly, while pouring a sporch and spinach surprise for a very short fairy with an unusually long nose.

'Well, apparently it was seen going through the windows of the blue house, you know, the one with the wishing well. It seems to have zoomed in and out of there so fast that it caught the curtains alight!'

'How can something move that fast? It can't be anything from Mirvellon – it's got to be from the other side, surely,' I said.

'And,' Bessie added, 'as it emerged from the window, it crashed straight into a pilp collector. They're bringing her here and they should be arriving, ooh, right about now!'

She pointed out of the window to a large crowd of fairies who were flying in towards the juice bar. They landed just outside the door forming a small circle four fairies deep. From the centre came a terrible howling and wailing.

'I-I-I thought it was a firefly but it was too bright for that and too quick. It was whizzing in and out of the windows before I had chance to collect ...' A whimpering sigh indicated that the speaker had fainted.

'Here,' came a gravelly voice, 'give her some of this juice, it'll make her feel a little ... better.'

An anonymous hand thrust a grey bottle into the crowd. It was passed through to the fairy who drank it gratefully and drained its contents.

'Give her air, give her air,' shouted Fred.

'Well, what do you make of that Bess? ' I turned and caught her in mid drool, looking dreamily in Fred's direction.

'Close your mouth, Bess. It's just Fred,' I said mockingly.

I moved in closer to get a better look at the victim.

'Bess,' I called, 'look who it is!'

It was Phyllis Router, a fairy of my age who was in my class at school. I say in my class loosely as her actually being in class was a rarity. Her mother often kept her at home to help look after the five smaller Routers so she only appeared on compulsory exam dates. Phyllis was also a well known teller of tall tales, an absolute out and out liar!

'I-I-I was so scared,' she sobbed, wiping the tears from her grubby face. She rubbed her hands nervously down her dress which used to be brown but was now grey, stained and ripped at the hem. She pushed her hair away from her eyes and tucked the remaining strands behind her small pointed ears.

'I-I-I tell you, it came straight at me. A light it was. And I dropped my bag of pilps because I was so scared,' she scratched anxiously at a bright red mark on her arm as she spoke.

'What else can you remember?' asked Fred. 'Was there any noise that came with it?'

Phyllis made several different sounds before bursting into tears once again.

'And exactly where did the alleged flash of light take place, Phyllis?' said Fred, taking a small, tatty notebook from his pocket.

'W-What?' said Phyllis.

'He means where did it all happen!' I called.

'I-It was just round the corner from the blue house,' Phyllis whimpered.

Hmm, that wasn't far from our spot. Not far from where I had seen the light last nightsgritch.

'I-I-I was so f-f-frightened. I-I didn't know what it was. I-I thought it was a Grublin, a f-fast flying Grublin.'

'Err, d-did she say G-Grublin, Aggie, did she?' called Bessie over the numerous fairy heads.

'No, she said she thought it was bubbling,' I called back. We already had one hysterical fairy, we certainly didn't need another.

'I-I was all on my own. It just came right at ...' she'd fainted again.

– 55 –

I pushed through the crowd to reach the limp and lifeless body, 'I think we'd better get her home.'

'I could take her,' said the gravelly voice from the back of the crowd.

'No,' said Fred. He looked round for the owner of the voice. 'I'll do it.'

'Well, do it quickly,' I whispered. 'She's looking positively grey.'

He tucked Phyllis firmly under his arm and flew off in the direction of the Router home.

'Oh, isn't he wonderful,' sighed Bessie, looking longingly after him.

'Crikey, Bess, is that all you can think about? What about poor Phyllis?'

'I'm sorry – he just looked so in control – you know,' she simpered.

'Oh, enough! I've got to get home. You coming?'

But before she could answer, a loud 'Ahem!' was directed my way.

'And just what am I supposed to do with him?' Mrs Cheric had a very purple Gilbert by the ear.

Whoops! Adverse effects!

******

Purple Gilbert was dropped home with profuse apologies and a tub of vanilla klupe to reverse the effects. Then it was Bessie's turn, leaving just me to fly the short distance home.

As I made my way, I was passed by some pilp collectors, their sacks full, also making their way home. My thoughts turned from Phyllis to Albert and I began to wonder how if he had actually made it out on the nightsgritch at all. Some ace collector he was!

Opening the door to our house, I soon discovered that Albert had been out but looking at the bag in the hallway, the results didn't look good. It wasn't that full and there seemed to be a hole in the corner … and it looked a bit burnt.

'What happened to the bag, Albert?' Pa asked.

'I'm not sure, Pa. I might have got caught on something I suppose. That's probably how I came to lose so many pilps along the way.'

I could hardly believe my pointed little ears. He had failed, once again, to bring home enough pilps. That meant more work for me and no credits for a new dress of any kind.

Not that I needed one now. I wouldn't be going to the pilpblast. I'd rather stay in and … read. Perhaps if I said this over and over before I fell asleep, I could really convince myself too.

******

I woke up earlier than usual, desperate to talk to Phyllis. I planned to call round to her house before going to school. Hopefully, she could shed some new light on *the light.*

Bugface was still sleeping, though not too soundly.

'Grublins! Grublins! Get them off, Get them off!' she shouted, her eyes still tightly closed, her arms thrashing around wildly.

'Wake up, Bugface. You're having another nightmare.' I gave her a *gentle* little shake.

She opened her eyes wide. 'What's going on?'

'Grublin nightmare – again!'

'Oh, sorry. Why are you up so early?' she said.

'I've got things to do.'

'Oh yeah, things that don't include 'stupid bugfaced sisters' – I know.' She fell back on her pillow and pulled the bedclothes over her head.

Time for an apology.

'I'm sorry, Myrtle. Something happened to me and I just took it out on you,' was the best kind of apology I could muster so early in the morning.

'I know. It's okay,' she said graciously, sitting up once more.

'It's good of you to say that.'

'No! I mean, I know! I know what happened to you. I was hoping you would tell me yourself that's why I kept asking.'

How did she know? Did I talk in my sleep?

'Ma said I needed to take some gentle exercise so I decided to come and meet you from school. I waited around the corner of the dress shop, opposite the

– 58 –

library hoping to surprise you. When Gertie Cruet came out clutching a bag and I saw you round the back of the library, I sort of put two and three together and got five.'

'So you also know I lied to Ma. I suppose you've told her everything, haven't you? I'm going to be in for it now. Ma hates liars.' I sunk back down on the bed.

'No, I didn't do or say anything. Well, I suppose that's not strictly true.'

'What do you mean? You haven't told anyone else have you? Please Myrtle! Leave me some dignity!'

'No, of course I haven't. No, I mean, to say I didn't do anything is not strictly true. I did do something.' She looked proudly at me. 'I did something for you.'

'So what *did* you do, Myrtle?'

She crawled around the floor, mimicking some strange creature.

'No more, please! What did you do?'

'Guess who set the web trap for Gertie Cruet?'

The web trap! She'd set the web trap for Gertie. My little sister had set the web trap for Gertie Cruet, arch enemy.

'You did that for me, Myrtle? That was a brilliant idea!'

And then we hugged, a strange and rare experience for us – and then we quickly unhugged! Uugghh!

'Why didn't you say so?' I said.

'I thought I just did,' Myrtle giggled. Then she asked the question I'd been dreading. 'What will you wear now, Aggie, to the pilpblast, I mean?'

'I've decided not to go to the pilpblast after all. I'm going to stay home ... and read,' I said.

'Read? But you can't do that Aggie! It's the most important time of the year. Everyone will be there!'

'Everyone will be there except me, who will be reading quietly at home.'

'You could wear the one you wore last year if we changed the collar or something.' She went to the wardrobe and took out the green dress. 'The pilpblast is still a month away. I could do it for you,' she went on.

'No, Myrtle, look,' I pulled the dress across my waist,' it's too tight. I said you could have it, remember? I've made my mind up. I'm staying home.'

That was my final word on the matter I decided. I had other things to think about now. The light! I needed to talk to Phyllis about the light.

'But Aggie ... ' she called.

'Bye – Bugface,' I said, lightly. 'See you later.' It was time to find out just how big a liar Phyllis really was.

Chapter Six

The house Phyllis lived in stood out from the rest. It was a darker shade of decay than the surrounding homes and it had less windows. Various bits of toys and a selection of balls littered the large front garden. An enormous clothes tree stood in the middle where the lawn once was. As always, its vast branches sagged heavily with wet washing – well, what would you expect with five fairylets?

After several painful knocks on the battered wooden door, it finally opened.

'Is Phyllis in?' I asked a small brother (or was it a sister?).

'Mum said she's not to be disturbed 'cos of last night,' said the brother-sister, picking bits of bread out of its hair.

'Well, it's about last night that I want to see her, perhaps if I just come in for a little while?' I pushed past the little brother-sister fairylet and let myself into the kitchen.

'Oh, it's you Aggie. Come to see Phyllis have you?' Mrs Router came to see who had been at the door. She was clutching a small fairylet, so young that its wings were still curled around its body.

'Yeah, would it be all right to see her? I won't stay long.'

'She's still a little shaken. I'm not sure she's up to a second visitor. She's got to rest up for the nightsgritch.' She sounded worried, not surprising as Phyllis was the only working collector in the family. Hang on. Did she say second visitor? Fred!

'It'ss okay, mum. Lett Aggie come throughh,' Phyllis lisped from the doorway.

She still looked a little odd, sort of, off colour, grey in colour in actual fact. It was probably the shock. She scratched nervously at her arm which was now swollen and blistered ... and also a little grey.

'So ... how've you been, huh?' I asked, trying to make polite conversation.

She didn't answer. She just stared at the floor.

'Err, do you mind if I ask you some questions about last night only I think it might be the same thing ...'

'It wass a bright fastt light,' she sighed, cutting me short. She'd obviously said it all before to Fred.

It sounded pretty familiar.

'What about size? What about colour?' Surely there must be more.

'Well, itt was a little taller thann you. I'm not sure of the colour. It wass yellowy-white.'

Most lights were!

'There did seemm like a fleck of colour, like a tinge to itt.'

What if it had been a reddish tinge? That could be a Great Molarite travelling at forty times the speed of light!! A bluish tinge could point the finger at an Incisortonian!! Also travelling at the very normal forty times the speed of light!

I looked at her arm, now swollen and oozing a clear liquid.

'How did you get that mark on your arm, Phyllis?'

She looked down at the floor, shuffled her feet and then looked directly at me and said, 'It wass the light. It burnt mee as it passed.'

'I should get it looked at by a healer, if I were you,' I said, feeling quite sorry for her by now.

I left the Routers with a scruffy note in my hand from Mrs Router for Miss Thrune. One more sick note for the growing volumes the school already held.

So many things Phyllis had said whizzed around in my head. Damn! It was all becoming far too complicated. It was so much simpler in the beginning. Bright light, fast. Bright light, fast.

Perhaps I might be able to think more clearly if someone would stop that flipping bell from ringing! Bell ringing? Oh great! I was late for school again. At least this time I had a note, albeit Phyllis Router's.

******

I arrived just in time to see the main door being slammed shut, causing the windows immediately above it to rattle furiously. Four little hands emerged to hold the frame in place.

I flew round to the side window which served as a sneak-in for latecomers. There was a bit of a queue yet I still managed to be inside shortly after the bell had stopped ringing. But my pleasure at being almost on time was hampered as I spotted Gertie Cruet and cronies in the corridor. Late and Gertie Cruet! Just flipping marvellous!

'Late again, Lichen. Whatever will Mr Fettock say?' she said mockingly.

I knew I'd have to face her but hadn't yet planned or practised any response to what she was obviously going to say.

'Ah, and she's got a note from her mummy,' Petunia chipped in. Gertie snorted loudly.

I needed to say something witty, something smart ... then I thought of Myrtle's web trap and I just couldn't help smiling as I pictured Gertie walking head on into a nest of spiders. Classic! What I would have given just to have been there to watch.

'What's she doing Petunia?' Gertie muttered, 'Why's she gone all ... smiley?'

She seemed to come over all unnecessary, giving a hysterical giggle as I, posing as the manic fairy from hell, walked past grinning menacingly. And the more I thought about the trap, the wider my smile became.

Well, with Gertie dealt with I now just had to get by Fettock's office and slip into class.

Miss Thrune would be looking for me at the window so I should be able to sneak in through the door without her noticing. That is unless she decided to look for me at the door instead!

Damn! Why do teachers do things like that? You know, do things out of character and at the wrong times.

'I do have a note this time though, Miss,' I pleaded.

'But this is about Phyllis Router. It's nothing to do with your lateness, Aggie.'

'I didn't say it was, Miss. I just said I had a note!'

I noticed a faint smile appear on her lips at my cheek. I decided not to push my luck and quickly found somewhere to perch.

A few stray looks and sniggers told me that Gertie Cruet had been at work spreading her cruel tales. Still, who cared? I had a deadly weapon now – a manic smile with teeth as optional extras.

I was still smiling, this time inwardly, when I noticed that Fred had yet to arrive at school. It was a full hour before he floated casually into class and sat himself down next to me.

'Where have you been, Fred? You were way ahead of me,' I whispered trying not to catch Miss Thrune's eye. She was desperately trying to explain the laws of aerodynamics to an unwilling and disinterested audience.

'... *and the harder you flap ...*'

'I just had some bits to do before class, that's all,' said Fred.

'... *the higher you will go ...*'

'You sound just like Albert. He's always got 'bits' to do or he's 'working' on something. I think it's just some grand excuse for being late,' I sneered.

'... *and the slower you flap ...*'

There was more to him than met the eye ... and he was just as secretive as Albert. Perhaps they were working on 'bits' together!

'... *the more chance you have of flapstopping ...*'

The lesson seemed to drag on forever. Surely all we needed to know was flap wings fast to move, flap wings slow to stop. Fast, slow, fast, slow, simple – you'd think.

The remainder of the morning passed quickly and I was grateful for that final bell so that I could get home. No nightsgritch for me tonight – I'd swapped with Albert. I was looking forward to going to the juice bar again with Bessie.

Unfortunately, when I arrived home I found that Ma had other plans for me – the nightsgritch! She wanted me to go out collecting to try and make up the credits we would be missing. Why me? Where the hell was Albert?

'But Ma, it's my night off. I've made plans. I'm meeting Bessie at the juice bar. I ...'

'Aggie, Albert's not around so I need you to go and besides, aren't you in need of some credits for your dress? You could take Bessie with you.'

'But Ma ...'

'Good, that's settled then.'

****

I knew Bessie wouldn't be allowed on the nightsgritch with me. Her mum was insistent on her getting enough wing rest. But I had a better idea. Fred! I'd ask Fred. He was off tonight. It'd give me a chance to talk to him about where he was earlier ... and about the light.

So that's how it ended up with me and Fred on a nightsgritch together. He said he was thinking of going anyway to gather a few extra pilps for the family. Now he would also help gather a few extra pilps for my family.

We chatted casually as we collected from the donors and the pilp sack started to bulge nicely. I began to feel relaxed again, finding comfort in the knowledge that this time I most certainly would have a pilp load to talk about. In fact things were going great until we reached the house next to the blue house with the wishing well in the front garden. Looking around it was hard to take in, as the trees

– 67 –

that surrounded us were all badly burnt. Wisps of black smoke were pouring from gaping holes and grey sticky gunge seeped despairingly from the open wounds. The trees were weeping. Their branches clawed wildly at the smouldering trunks in an effort to pat out the remaining flames that fed on their bark. It was a fearful sight.

'What the hell happened here?' I asked. 'I mean, this is no ordinary fire. See how high the marks are?' I pointed to the scorch marks high up on the tree trunks. 'And what's that awful smell?'

Fred sniffed the air.

'Pigging hell, Fred. It was Grublins. I'd bet my wings on it.'

'No ...'

'I can smell them, Fred. Nasty, vile creatures. They're probably still here, all around us, waiting for us to come out ...'

'No! This isn't the work of Grublins.' Fred shook his head in disbelief, 'It can only be one thing, Aggie – *the light*. It's obviously been this way.'

I looked around hoping to see the instigator of the chaos but could see nothing much through the putrid smoke. Fred had made his way to a silver tree that was fighting a losing battle against the flames but there was little he could do but hover and watch. Our size made it impossible to quench the flames in anyway at all.

'Fred, there's nothing we can do here. We have to move on.' I grabbed his arm and turned to leave.

'What's that noise, Aggie?'

'Fred, we really must go.'

'Listen!'

In the distance I could hear a slight buzzing, like the sound of an annoying fly! It stopped just as suddenly as it had started. Fred and I looked at each other. Then, moving just beyond the trees was a light, a bright flickering light. Could this be it? Could this be *the light*?

Chapter Seven

We flew swiftly through the smouldering trees, covering our mouths so as not to inhale the smoke. The buzzing sound had grown louder now and seemed to be all around us. Tears streamed from my throbbing eyes as the smoke swirled and thickened. There seemed to be no escape.

'I think we're done for,' said Fred.

I wiped my eyes and scanned around. There had to be some way out of here.

'Quick, make for that gap,' I said, pointing to a space between two large branches. Fresh air filled our lungs as we swept through. And after a short spell of coughing and spluttering, followed by a longer spell of swearing and cursing, we both felt much better. We had emerged into a small untidy back yard, littered with toys – the big house with the red door!

Whoosh!

Fred ducked as the light passed overhead. He grabbed my arm roughly and pulled me back behind a wall so that we couldn't be seen. The light was clearly going in and out of the windows and at a tremendous speed too. Fred began to rummage through his pockets.

'Hell, Fred, this is no time to look for a snack. That light thing might see or hear us. We'll be charcoal'

'Actually, I was looking for my picturetaker. I brought it with me just in case.' And with that he leaned around me and began snapping.

'We're really going to have to move from here soon, Fred, or we'll miss the exit,' I said after a while.

Fred nodded in agreement and packed the picture-taker away again. Peering out from behind the wall, the way seemed clear so we made our escape and started towards home. We hadn't gone far when a startled scream stopped us in our tracks. We looked at each other. *The light!* It must have paid somefairy a visit.

'We can't just leave, Fred. What if somefairy's hurt?'

'If we don't go now we'll both be hurt. Correction! We'll be more than hurt, we'll be dead!'

'Fine, you go on. Take the pilps to Ma. I'm going back.' I was half hoping he'd come with me but he'd gone, out of sight, vanished!

The screaming now seemed to come from far below me. There was only one way to find the owner of the scream and get us both to the exit before the sun rose; flapstopping! Dangerous, absolutely. Foolish, most definitely. Necessary, yes, completely! It was the only way. The problem was it wasn't something fairies actually practised, quite the opposite in fact. At school we practised how *not* to flapstop!

This was scary stuff indeed. My heart was near to bursting it was beating so fast. What was I doing?

I didn't even know who was down there. I had to do it.

I spread my wings as wide as possible and began the flapstopping process.

Flap, flap, flap, flap, flap, flap.

Stopppppppp!

'Aaaaaaaahhhhhhhhhhhhhhhhhhh.'

I started to plummet sharply towards the ground gathering speed as I fell. My ears popped from the pressure but I felt the source of the scream get nearer. I had to concentrate. I had to get it just right. If I left it too late I would become a splat on the landscape, a squashed berry for the birds to pick at. Ugh! Let's not go there!

The screams were getting louder and louder, a good indication that I was close. Time for some speedy flapping of the wings if I was to avoid being ground splattered. I said time for some *speedy* flapping. Pigging hell! It was much harder than I thought. I urged my wings to flap harder but they didn't quite seem to get the message.

Flaaaap, flaaaap, flaaaap.

Oooohhhhhh!

Wings ache!

Back sore!

Must flap harder.

Flaap, flaap, flaap.

Wings ache!

Back sore!

Feel faint!

Head rush!

Must flap harder. Flaaap, flaaap, flaaap.

Ground splattering approaching fast.

Goodbye cruel world.

I landed with a hefty thump. Everything was dark. Everything was black. Everything was … sticky. Not sticky in the gooey sense but sticky as in sticks. I'd landed face down in an empty birds nest. The end had passed me by. I brushed myself down, rubbing my knees which were grazed and bleeding and hauled myself to the edge of the nest. The screaming was loud and clear and, by the sound of it, coming from the next tree. I was exhausted and as hard as I tried, I just couldn't gather enough power to project myself the short distance to the other tree – and time was running out, the exit wouldn't stay open for much longer. I would have to try to leap across and flap at the same time. It was all I had. I took a run from the back of the nest and jumped high and wide across the gap, flapping frantically at the same time. But it wasn't enough. My wings just collapsed wearily and I began once more to plummet to the ground. My life began to unfold before me as I prepared to meet my maker. I could see events from the past. I could see my friends. I could see Bessie. I could see Fred. In fact, I could see Fred very clearly indeed.

'Did you really think I'd leave you to get all the

glory?' he said, grabbing hold of me tightly and smiling.

For once in my life I was speechless. Talking was going to take a while anyway seeing as I had little breath to breathe with let alone speak with.

As we moved upwards I started to feel a little better. Less light headed. Less almost dead!

My mind starting thinking again. The screamer! What about the screamer?

'I found the screaming fairy on the way down to you. She's perched a little further upwards. We'll pick her up on the way.'

Fred had read my mind, which must have been a little tricky seeing as it felt as if it had been scrambled and put through the wringer!

Sure enough the screaming fairy was on a branch a little higher only she wasn't screaming anymore, she was crying instead.

I couldn't believe my eyes. It was Phyllis Router – again. 'Crikey, Phyllis, you must be the unluckiest fairy ever.'

Fred, however, was less sympathetic and launched straight into a question and answer session. 'I know you're frightened but I may be able to help if you tell me exactly what happened to you,' said Fred. 'How on earth did you end up down there anyway?'

'Well, I was just going about my business, collecting pilps as one does ...'

I interrupted urgently, 'Look, I hate to break up

this lovely chit-chat but I do believe we've got an exit to catch!'

Fred looked up at the sky. 'Oh, hell, we're nearly out of time. Phyllis, climb on my back and hold on tight.'

We flew for our lives, pushing our wings to their limits as we soared towards the exit. As the colours of dawn started to break across the sky, the door appeared within our sights. It would be touch and go if we made it in time. Then, to our surprise the door opened as if a miracle had happened to allow us to pass through quicker. Tasheena, the fairy goddess, had smiled down on us – and opened the door? Well that would have been very kind of her but I suspected greater forces were at work here. Ah! Did I say greater forces? How about miserable, moaning forces? Gilbert!

He had been hanging around the exit waiting for Fred and he had some very important news to share with us. His bespectacled face was as miserable as ever, his timing impeccable.

'I'm afraid I've got some bad news,' he began solemnly, his head hanging down sorrowfully. 'It's *really, really* bad, Fred.' Gilbert's face contorted as if in complete agony.

'Well, it'll have to keep, Gilbert. We've got to get Phyllis home first. She's had rather a nasty shock,' said Fred.

'Well, I've got *rather a nasty shock* for you all as

well,' he raised his voice impatiently. 'You see ...'

'Gilbert, I think Phyllis has had enough for one day. Keep your shock a little longer – that'll give you time to embellish the facts a little!'

Fred beckoned to me, still insisting that we flew Phyllis home.

'I'll have to drop the pilps into Ma first, Fred ...'

'It's okay, Aggie. Gilbert will drop them in on his way home. It'll keep him busy.' Gilbert stamped his foot in frustration as Fred shoved the pilp sack into his reluctant arms.

'But Fred I've got ...'

'Gilbert, what you've got is a bag of pilps to deliver to Aggie's mum, now go, and no more buts!' Fred pointed in the direction of my house and at last the reluctant fairy took off into the sky.

'I'm sure he's getting worse, Fred. He never seems to stop moaning these days,' I said, taking hold of Phyllis' arm.

Fred nodded and smirked, 'That's just what my mum said. Why she doesn't use ear plugs like me and dad I just don't know!'

Ear plugs! So that's how everyone else coped with Gilbert and his moaning. I must add them to my shopping list. They could go under the word 'dress' which was now scribbled out.

****

Phyllis didn't live that far away but she chatted enough to fill in the little time we had before we reached her house.

'It started with a faint noise, just like before, you know, like in the distance,' she began.

'What kind of noise, though? What did it sound like?' urged Fred.

'Well it was kind of strange. At first I thought it was an annoying fly sound so I didn't take too much notice …'

She then went on to describe, in great detail, how she had first heard the buzzing noise.

'It was like the noise in the pilp plant, you know where the pilps become energy. Yeah, that's what it sounded like.' She nodded, quietly confident. 'There was one other thing – a really nasty smell, kind of sewer smell. It was around at the same time as the light.'

A light that not only burned anything it touched but also possibly smelled like a sewer! An interesting combination but at last we had something new to go on, what with the pictures Fred had taken. We should be well on our way to solving the light mystery. Shouldn't we?

Fred continued to question Phyllis. It turned out that the light had whizzed passed her so quickly that she'd lost her balance, flapstopped and fell. And I thought it was only after me!

'If it wasn't for that tree ... I'd have been bird fodder,' she said sadly as if reliving the moment.

Physically, apart from a small tear in her left wing and a few bruises, she was fine. But her pilp sack was lost – something which was now becoming a regular occurrence where the light was involved.

Before long we arrived at Phyllis' house.

'Oh my portals above! Not again, Phyllis. You poor thing ... and no pilps collected either. Oh dear!' said Mrs Router as we met her at the door. 'You should have just sent a message via dragonfly, Fred. I'd have come and met you – saved you the trouble.'

'But she was in a right state. We just needed to get her home,' said Fred.

'Well, I'm that grateful to you for seeing to my Phyllis. I ain't got much but you're welcome to a nice bottle of juice for the flight home.' She took two grey bottles from behind the door and thrust them into our hands.

'Bye ... and thank you.' Mrs Router then disappeared inside with Phyllis.

'You do realise what'll be waiting for us,' I said, reminding Fred of Gilbert's *really nasty shock.*

Fred smirked. 'Best not keep him waiting too long then.'

We took off and headed towards Incisorton. As we flew over the pilp plant, we could just make out a small, sombre clad figure pacing the path outside Fred's house. Gilbert ran to greet us as we landed, almost knocking Fred off his feet.

'Where've you been, Fred? I've been waiting hours to tell you …' he began.

'Then you won't mind waiting a couple more minutes while I put these bottles in the fridge, will you?' He grabbed the grey bottle from my hand and disappeared inside the house. He emerged a few minutes later smiling broadly.

'Now little fairy, what of this terrible news!'

'Cruet's selling the pilp plant,' said Gilbert, groaning heavily.

'Cruet's *selling* the pilp plant?' Fred repeated.

'That's what I just said.'

'How can Cruet sell the pilp plant? It's not his to sell. It's supposed to be a community pilp plant.'

'And there's more.'

'Well, go on then, spit it out.' Fred was growing more impatient by the minute.

'He's selling it to Arty Granger, you know, he lives in Great Molaring.'

Yes, we knew Arty Granger all right, he ran with Grublins. Rumour had it that he spent so much time with them that he was beginning to look like one.

'Are you sure about this? I mean, where would somefairy like Arty find enough credits for that? You'd better not be taking the …' I shouted.

'I'm not … it's all true. Gertie Cruet's been telling everyfairy about it. She's going to be rich!'

'What about Ferret? Has anyone spoken to him

about it? He'd know what Arty was up to,' said Fred.

Ferret Granger, fairykin of Arty, was one of the wealthiest and meanest fairies around. He got his nickname because of the amount of pilps he'd ferreted away over the years, and because he was a Great Molarite this amounted to a huge number of credits.

'He's not in town at the moment,' said Gilbert. 'He's away on urgent business, Mrs Yewster said.'

Sounded a little too convenient to me.

'Well, perhaps somefairy ought to send him a dragonfly,' I stood with my hands firmly placed on my hips. 'Let him know that there's urgent business here too!'

'... or perhaps you ought to just go home before your mum sends a dragonfly for you.' Fred laughed at my stance, 'Haven't you got a nightsgritch tonight?'

'Oh, hell. I forgot about that. Ma will do me if I don't get back on time,' I said relaxing once more.

A titter came from behind me. 'And you can shut that giggling up too, Gilbert Trickle.'

Hell, what a day this had been. What did it all mean?

Questions formed in the back of my mind. What I hadn't realised yet was how the answers were unfolding all around me.

Chapter Eight

I was eager to see if the pictures Fred took of the light were ready so I decided to call on him a couple of days later.

Bessie had decided to come too. 'You're not going to be talking about the light all the time, are you?'

'Well, it was quite dramatic, Bess. It was so close to us and it set the woods on fire and poor Phyllis was in quite a state and ...'

'Blah, blah, blah. Boring! Is that all you can talk about? What about the pilpblast? Can't we talk about that? You're still going aren't you? Do you want to know what I'm wearing?' With that amount of questions, Bessie managed to sidetrack the initial conversation successfully and hooked me straight in.

'Okay, okay! What are you wearing?' I conceded.

And so the conversation for the rest of the journey centred on the pilpblast and what Bessie would be wearing. By the time we arrived at Fred's house, I felt totally pilpblasted out!. At last we could talk about something different – the pictures.

'Hey, Fred. How's it going?' Bessie enquired, as he opened the door. She stood there twisting her plaits round her fingers.

'I was just having a look at the pictures I took the other night to see if anything was familiar. They're a bit blurry. What do you think?' said Fred, scratching his head.

Would you like me to take a look, Fred?' said Bessie, snatching the pictures out of his hand. She flicked quickly through. 'Hmm, nothing much here. Nothing at all in fact.'

'Oh, give them here.' I grabbed them from her and scanned quickly through the pictures. She was right. There wasn't that much to see. A flash of light was in each one but little else was visible to the naked eye.

'We'll just have to try again, Fred. I'm sure if we wait long enough …'

'Oh, blah, blah, blah! Here we go again!' complained Bessie. She held her hands over her pointy ears in disgust.

If only she'd have been there. Then she'd have realised how important this could be.

'Why don't you take the pictures, Aggie?' said Fred. 'You've got a glass and water enlarger, haven't you?'

I nodded and tucked the pictures away in my bag.

Perhaps that might reveal a clue or two to the identity of the light.

'I'll let you know …' I was interrupted by Gilbert who stormed into the room waving his arms around.

The door almost bounced off its hinges.

'I've got some news! I've got some news!' he screamed. His thick black glasses almost fell off his nose as he grinned excitedly.

Fred sprayed his hair with water and attempted to flatten down his crown tuft. 'So what did you find out?'

'Well, Mrs Yewster, in the store, she said that there was a contract made exactly one hundred years ago between Mr Cruet's ancestors and Pilpsville Community Council.'

'Yes and ...' said Fred, impatiently.

'Well, Mrs Yewster, in the store, she said the contract gave over the ownership of the plant to Mr Cruet if, after one hundred years, the plant was still being run by a member of the Cruet family.'

'Pigging hell! This is bad.' The flattened crown tuft shot back up, just as spiky as ever.

'Apparently Mr Cruet had come across the signed contract when he was extending Gertie's bedroom.'

Oh yes, we'd all heard about his new plans to include a walk-in wardrobe, if you please!

Hell! It would have been bad enough if Mr Cruet owned it but to then sell it to Arty Granger! Well, that was a different matter. Somehow, he had single handedly found enough credits to buy the plant outright. No one knew how. He had rarely been seen on a nightsgritch.

'If we're going to stop Arty Granger buying the pilp plant, we're all going to have to pull together as a community. The lifestyle of every fairy in Pilpsville depends on it.'

Fred was at it again. He stopped suddenly and looked at me.

'So what's the plan then?' he said eagerly, a manic look on his face.

'Well, I thought we could ...' I began.

'Excuse me. Plan? What do you mean, plan? What about the pilpblast???' Bessie showed further signs of dismay through an embarrassing show of grunting and sighing. All of which was quickly ignored.

'I think it's time for a meeting, a community meeting. Somefairy had better go and ring the fire bell,' I said, taking charge of the situation.

As the bell continued to ring, the tooth fairy community gathered in force, chatting loudly, wondering where the fire was. Fairies from all over Pilpsville were now assembling. From Great Molaring and Premolam they came, over the hill, past the school. Others from Incisortonian and Canningford were approaching fast. It was a wondrous sight. I could feel a great speech rising in me as I stood to address the bulging crowd of ... eleven!!

'Is this it?' I exclaimed bitterly. 'Tooth fairies united!'

'Well yes and no, everyone's gone to the school hall. The meeting's going to be in there,' said Bessie.

'Hurry up if you're coming,' and off she flew.

So much for my great idea.

'So who exactly is running this meeting then?' I enquired as we reached the entrance to the hall.

Once inside, however, my question was answered. Fettock! Blooming Fettock. I should have known. There he stood on the stage for all to see. Fettock! Fist in the air, saying how Cruet and Arty shouldn't get away with it! Fettock, calling for proof of Mr Cruet's ownership certificate! Fettock!

Actually his speech was quite good.

'We'll need all families to pull together. If we can raise enough credits we could buy the pilp plant from Mr Cruet,' he said.

'Why should we? It's not really his to sell,' came a shout from the crowd.

'Yeah, why should we line his wings with silver?' screamed another fairy.

Mr Fettock gestured for calm, 'I can't see that we have much choice! If we all chip in ...'

The trouble was, whatever they were asking for, we didn't have it. I could see Ma and Pa sitting near the back squirming and looking very uncomfortable. A few faces turned in their direction, then turned back, mouthing words to one another. Cheek!

'We've barely got enough credits for ourselves,' whispered Ma to Pa. He patted Ma's hand and told her not to worry.

It was no secret that our family was having credit

problems. Things had certainly gone downhill in the last few weeks, what with Myrtle's flapstopping performance and Albert's sudden inability to collect enough pilps or, indeed, Albert's inability to be visible at any given time. Where was he now, I wondered? Why was he never around lately? But I wasn't the only one looking for answers; Phyllis's mum also had a question to ask.

'But what about that light, shouldn't we be sorting that out first.' A very angry Mrs Router stood up and addressed the crowd, a fairylet tucked under one arm. 'We've lost three sacks of pilps so far.' – I could have sworn it was just two – 'When's that going to be dealt with, huh?'

Phyllis sat quietly as her mother spoke and pulled the scarf she was wearing closer to her face. She still looked a little grey to me and had obviously been crying as her eyes were glazed and bulging. She hung her head as her mother returned to her seat.

'We haven't got time to deal with some flying glow worm,' shouted a very short fairy from the back of the hall. A long nose protruded from behind it's oversized hood.

'Yeah, we've more important things ...' said another.

'But look what it did to my poor Phyllis,' Mrs Router yanked Phyllis up and uncovered her red and blistered arm for all to see. 'Twice it's attacked, twice!'

– 86 –

Gasps went up from the crowd.

'Yeah, and what about all those pilp sacks being lost because of this light? No pilps, no credits,' another voice chipped in.

'But we've got to save the pilp plant first. After all, it's our livelihood.' It was the very short fairy again.

There followed a great deal of debate. Mrs Router continued her rally on Phyllis' behalf but it was eventually decided that the selling of the pilp plant by Mr Cruet was top priority, not some so-called low flying glow worm/fluorescentdragonfly/bad-tempered bluebottle/angry firefly or such like.

'Who was that short fairy at the back, Ma? I didn't recognise him at all,' I asked quietly as we left the hall.

'Don't know, Aggie,' she muttered, 'I just don't know.'

She wasn't interested in what I had said. She had her own worries. I followed behind meekly.

The silent procession continued and I was more than pleased to reach home and the comfort of my bedroom. Of course Myrtle was already in there, spread across the bed, waiting to hear what all the fuss was about.

'What happened at the meeting? Was there lots of arguing and shouting?' she asked.

'Nah, not much,' I said, dismissively. 'Where's Albert?'

'He had to go out for a while. He said he won't be too long,' she said. 'Now what about the meeting?'

I left Ma to deal with her endless questions while I went in search of the glass and water enlarger. I needed to get a closer look at those pictures. It was somewhere in the house but where?

'Where did you last see it?' asked Pa innocently.

Isn't that just a classic? 'Where did you last see it?' Surely if you knew where you last saw it, it wouldn't be lost and you wouldn't be looking for it in the first place!

The only place I hadn't looked was Albert's room. Trouble was, it was usually locked, but being a little sister is all about knowing where your big brother keeps the key of course. Small stool required for height, then just need to poke my finger in the crack above his bedroom door and ... bingo!

The key turned easily in the lock and the door fell open to reveal the contents of a big brother's bedroom. Blimey, and I thought my room was messy! Albert, when actually in, obviously wasn't one for tidying up it seemed. Apart from the normal assortment of clothes, both clean and dirty I suspected, scattered on the floor and the bed, there were pieces of metal and a variety of tools. Empty cups and plates littered the floor and a rubbish bin in the corner overflowed with screwed up paper. Nothing unusual you'd think, but on the desk were pieces of paper with drawings on them, some sort of plans from what I could make out. What they were for I couldn't quite say. Mmm, some kind of tubes strapped together. If I could just move the paper round I could get a better idea of what it was. Ah ha! No better in actual fact! Perhaps if I just tilted it …

'Aggie!'

to the left …

'Aggie!!'

or to the right …

'Aggie!!! I've found it,' Pa shouted impatiently. 'Ma had it in the bedroom. I was just talking to Albert about it when she remembered …'

Albert!!! Damn.

I quickly returned the paper back in its place and tiptoed to the door. There was just time to lock the door quickly and return the key to the crack above the door. Phew!

'Hey, Albert. How's it going?' I said, strolling casually into the kitchen.

'What have you been up to? You'd better not have been in my room.'

'L-L-Like how could I? It's always locked. Anyway, what are you hiding in there, huh?' I shifted the conversation back to Albert effortlessly.

Albert became strangely defensive. 'You just keep out, right?'

Pa interrupted and ended any further heated exchange of words between us.

'Here it is, Aggie. What'd you want it for?' Pa

handed me the enlarger.

'Oh, just to examine some pictures a little closer.'

'What pictures? Show me,' barked Albert.

Now he was interested in my life? I ignored him completely and went back to my room. Myrtle followed me in and sat on my bed.

'Shift, Bugface. I've got things to do.'

'Oh, let's have a look too, Aggie. After all, I was there when it first appeared,' she pleaded.

'Okay, just keep quiet about what you see, right?' Especially with Albert acting so strangely, I added to myself.

We sifted through the pictures carefully one by one, taking turns to examine them closely with the enlarger, and much was revealed …

…a thumbnail apparently belonging to Fred, the pink flowery wallpaper of the blue house pilp donor's bedroom, and a rather good close up of the red brick wall we hid behind!

It was hopeless. We knew no more than we had before. No, tell a lie, we knew that the blue house owners had terrible taste in wallpaper!

'This green light makes the pictures strange,' Myrtle said, waving a picture in front of my face.

'Mmmm, yeah, sure.'

'Are you listening? The green light has a funny affect on the pictures,' cried Myrtle impatiently, 'look!'

'What? How does that help?'

'I just meant that it shows up different shapes, all fuzzy like,' she went on.

'Give me the lamp, Myrtle. Let me look for myself.'

She passed me the bedside lamp that had been a twelfth birthday present from Great Aunt Wilma. I'd really liked it much. Too old fashioned for me. The green light that the bulb gave out had healing powers she had said. Hopefully, it had revealing powers too!

I placed a picture under the light.

'What can you see?'

'Nothing really,' I said with more than a hint of disappointment in my voice.

'Nothing? You must be able to see something,' she implored.

I held the picture closer to the light and screwed my eyes up to focus in more carefully. There in the top corner of the picture was something familiar. They looked like ... wings! It was more than just wings though. Fairy wings with a blue tinge to them, the unmistakable mark of an Incisortonian tooth fairy, one of our own! This I didn't share with Myrtle. I needed to follow up some of my own ideas about this first. One of our own but who?

'What can you see?' Bugface nudged me hard in the back.

I couldn't tell her everything. I needed to see Fred

and show him what I'd found but I had a strange feeling about it all, something I couldn't quite describe. I felt uneasy but I didn't know why.

I fobbed Bugface off with some old tale about it looking very similar to a firefly ... with a face! She wasn't terribly happy, but as I got ready for the nightsgritch – again – her happiness wasn't my concern. There were greater things at risk here and I still had that anxious, uneasy feeling about the light mystery and the pilp plant problem. My gut feeling told me that they were somehow connected. But how? And why? My mind went back to one of Myrtle's questions to Ma. 'Is something or somefairy helping Arty Granger to get the credits?'

They say every picture tells a story ...

Chapter Nine

Fred wasn't in school for the next couple of days.

'He's got wing rot, Lichen. Not that it's any of your business!' Miss Thrune had barked when asked of his whereabouts. 'Now get on with your embroidery. That sack's not going to sew itself.'

Bessie had other ideas though. 'Something's wrong at home,' she whispered. 'His mum's been seen acting very oddly.'

'But what about the pictures? I need him to look at them,' I moaned.

'Well, perhaps Fred could do with a visit to cheer him up!' She winked craftily. 'We'll go after school.'

****

We turned up on Fred's doorstep clutching the usual tatty handmade card signed by the whole class, except for Mildred Coinage, who'd fled to the toilet when wing rot was mentioned.

'They've closed all the curtains, Aggie. You don't think he's dead, do you?' Bessie asked, a hint of concern filling her voice.

I gave her a look and pulled on the door chime.
BOING!!

There was no answer. I yanked at the cord

again. A small door immediately above the chime was finally flung open. A tiny blue and extremely grumpy door gnome appeared. He was pinching his nose tightly.

'Whaja want?' he screeched.

'We're here to see Fred,' I said.

'No one in!' He slammed the tiny door shut again.

'Try again, Aggie,' said Bessie impatiently, poking me in the arm.

BOING!!

The tiny door flew open once more.

'I told you. No one in. Now you go away.' Bessie quickly caught the door before he had time to shut it again.

'Tell Fred we're here!' I said, pushing my face up to his.

'Okay, Okay, I tell him but you be sorry...' He disappeared inside and shut the tiny door firmly behind him.

After a few seconds Fred's mother appeared at the door. She seemed a little reluctant to let us in. She held a large white hankie in front of her mouth. Her eyes were turned downwards to her apron, which she started smoothing nervously with her spare hand.

'H-He's busy, come back at the weekend,' she mumbled, making a move to shut the door.

'But I really need to see him. It's urgent,' I pleaded.

We could hear raised voices in the background and, at the same time, the sound of footsteps running through the house. Mrs Trickle's head darted back and forth as she tried to deal with us and whatever was happening inside.

'I-I-I really can't ...' she turned back again and shouted loudly down the hall.

There was a sudden sound of something crashing to the ground.

'Oh, now what's he done? Look, just call back ...' Her head swivelled back round to the hall.

'Perhaps we can help?' Bessie looked at me, raising her eyebrows and nodding towards the door. I had no idea what she was letting us in for but Fred was in there and I needed to see him.

'Oh, come on then but don't say I didn't warn you.'

She opened the door a little wider and then pushed us into the living room. There was a really horrible smell hanging in the air. It was foul, just like a heap of rotten vegetables.

Bessie looked at me then whispered, 'Wing rot?'

I shrugged my shoulders.

Fred's mother looked rather embarrassed and ushered us through once more, this time into the kitchen. The smell followed like a loyal friend. It was becoming stronger and resembled more of a stench than a smell now.

'Quick', she said quietly, 'when I give you the nod,

run for the bathroom. Put a towel under the door so he can't get in.'

So *he* can't get in? Strange! Didn't she mean *it*? And why did we have to run from a smell?

She gave the nod and obediently, Bessie and I ran for the bathroom, shut the door quickly and placed a towel under the door.

Now what?

Bessie glared at me. 'What the heck's going on here, Aggie?' she said in a low voice.

'Like I know, Bess. I've just got here, how about you?' I whispered back and gave her an evil look but was interrupted by a gentle tap at the bathroom door. Accompanying this was a faint voice.

'It's me, Fred. Let me in quickly before he comes back.'

I pulled the towel away and flung the door open.

'AAArrgghh, what a rotten pong!' I said as we emerged from the safe cover of the bathroom.

'Damn! I almost had him trapped.' Fred stood on the other side of the door holding a jar in one hand and a lid in another. He looked a bit hacked off!

'Would somebody please tell me what the hell is going on? I only came to talk to you about the pictures, Fred, and I end up in some kind of foul-smelling nightmare.'

'Gilbert!' said Fred.

'What?' Bessie and I said together.

'Gilbert's what's going on. Old Skifle, the healer, got so sick of hearing him moan that she turned him into a flipping smell. It's supposed to give him a taste of his own medicine, you know, instead of Gilbert moaning and groaning, we do the moaning and groaning about him. I don't know who's suffering most though, him or us. Well *say* something!'

I looked at Bessie, she looked at me. Our reaction was the same.

'Ha, ha, ha.'

'Nice one Fred, very funny. Now tell us what's really going on,' Bessie added, still laughing at the prospect of a smelly, moaning, groaning Gilbert. Good grief, what could be worse than that?

'Quick, into mum's bedroom. Shut the door behind you and block the gap under the door. Come on, hurry before he comes back.' Fred seemed serious and was quite desperate to avoid the dreadful smell that was known in fairy form as Gilbert.

The problem was that Bessie and I thought it was all really funny. So funny, that we could hardly contain ourselves. I had to put my hand over my mouth and look away from Bessie in order to stop myself from laughing.

'You could hire him out, Fred. He could do house clearance!' she giggled, holding her stomach.

'Or how about pest control? He could drive them out with his smell.' That was it, I was no longer in control of my body, my sides were literally splitting and my legs were quickly crossed.

Fred, clearly not amused, pushed us into the room, quite roughly I might add.

'Oh come on Fred, lighten up. I mean, Gilbert the smell!' I laughed. 'It'll make a nice change from his moaning,' I added mockingly, closing the bedroom door behind us.

'You have him if it's such a *nice* change. It's alright for you two. You don't have to put up with it, do you?' said Fred irritably. He pushed a large blue towel under the bedroom door.

'It can't be for too much longer, surely. Just how long will he be like this?' Bessie asked, stifling a giggle successfully.

'Well, it's supposed to wear off after a couple of days but I don't know if we can cope that long.'

Then I thought of a brilliant idea.

'I've got a brilliant idea,' I said, 'but first we will need to capture Gilbert in the jar.'

Fred's mouth shot open. 'Doh! And what do you think *I've* been trying to do?' He shoved the jar and lid in my face for added effect.

He was right though. It wasn't going to be an easy task. What we needed was bait. Something to entice Gilbert into the jar, something to make him want to get in the jar, something or ... somefairy – Bugface!

I explained to Fred and Bessie, both of whom were holding their noses tightly at this point.

'Dat dounds dreat,' Bessie said. Loosely translated it meant that she thought it just might work.

Fred let go of his nose and moved towards the bedroom window. 'I'll send a dragonfly to get her,'

He whistled loudly and before too long, Corky the dragonfly appeared. Fred quickly scribbled a note to Myrtle and placed it in the message holder around Corky's neck.

'Right, now go find Myrtle,' shouted Fred, pointing in the direction of my house. The dragonfly spread his wings and flew off gracefully.

Knowing that it might be gone for some time, I began to explain my brilliant idea. It wasn't received as well as I had hoped.

'So what you're saying is, we let Gilbert out, having only just captured him, and the smell should clear the pilp plant so that we can get in and look at Mr Cruet's contract, which he's probably hidden away so that fairies like us can't find it?' Bessie said.

'So much negativity, guys. Come on, positive thinking now. It could just work, I mean look how he's made us run from room to room.'

'I agree …' said Fred.

'See, I told you it was a brilliant idea!' I threw a smug look across the room to Bessie.

'No, I agree with Bessie. If we do manage to pot Gilbert, the last thing we want to do is release him again, after all, look at the damage he's done so far.'

'Okay, so Gilbert the smell has made your mum throw up in the garden pond and made us retreat behind closed doors. That just shows you how effective he could be. We just have to control him, you know, have Myrtle – bribed obviously – standing near by when we want to recapture him.'

There was a sudden loud, frantic knocking on the bedroom door. This was accompanied by much spluttering and coughing. Myrtle had arrived.

'Let me in! Quickly, let me in!' she pleaded.

Fred pulled up the towel and inched open the door. Myrtle fell through the gap and landed in a heap on the bedroom floor.

'Blimey, you never said it was that bad, Fred,' exclaimed Myrtle getting herself to her feet.

'You mean, him not it – don't you?' said Bessie.

'Oh, for crying out loud, we're only talking about Gilbert and after what he did to mum I don't know why you're sticking up for him,' Fred said sharply. 'Now can we concentrate on getting HIM in the jar, please?'

And so the trap was set. Myrtle was prodded, pushed and placed in the doorway, reluctantly holding the jar and lid behind her back. The rest of us hid behind the door. Not a sound was heard, not a word was uttered, well not if you discount the mumblings Myrtle made under her breath.

Then a faint stinky whiff fell under our noses, passing backwards and forwards to each of us in turn. More of him appeared in the form of a stronger stinky smell, like that of old socks this time, and again it moved in front of us one by one. It – he – hadn't appeared to notice the bait, Myrtle, yet. But the worst was to come. It was the stinkiest, smelliest, most foul odour ever imagined and it – he – had wrapped itself – himself – around all of us. It was too much.

'Eeerrgghh,' Fred ran to the window, flung it wide open and coughed fiercely.

'Uuugghh,' Bessie started heaving and threw herself flat on the floor where, she reckoned, there was more oxygen.

So now I was left to somehow help Myrtle with the capture while preventing myself from being sick in Fred's waste-bin. It was a sight that begged for the presence of a picture taker!

Then it happened and, thankfully for us, it happened to Myrtle. She had been noticed by Gilbert at last and this time he didn't want to ask her to the pilpblast! It wasn't a pretty sight though, watching as she squirmed and wriggled then heaved as he came closer to her.

'AArrgghh, he's gone down my back. Get him out!' she yelled frantically.

'Hold the jar out, Myrtle,' called Fred from the window.

'AArrgghh,' she shrieked.

'Put one of your hair ribbons in the jar, you know,

something personal to attract him,' I shouted from the inside of the waste bin.

'AARRGGHH!'

'Oh give it here,' Bessie pulled herself up from the floor. She snatched the jar from Myrtle's hand and shouted loudly into the air, 'If you don't get yourself in the jar this instance Gilbert Trickle, I shall tell the whole school about that thing you did at the last pilpblast. You didn't really think I'd forget, did you?'

There was a sound like a gush of wind that flew around the room a few times, knocking several books and magazines off the shelf to the floor. It circled once more then flew out of the room, returning as quick as it had left.

'In Gilbert – NOW!' screamed Bessie, and the yellow wisp obeyed.

Snap! She pushed the lid down hard onto the jar.

'Phew!' she exclaimed as she fell back heavily on Fred's bed.

We all heaved a sigh of relief and sucked in large breaths of fresh air. At last, Gilbert the smell was contained and rendered harmless.

Now time to put the second part of my brilliant plan into action.

With Gilbert stored securely in the jar we decided to head off to the pilp plant.

'Thank you all so much, especially you Myrtle.' A grateful Mrs Trickle thrust several pieces of conka cake into our hands as we passed by her.

'Oh, it was nothing really, Mrs Trickle,' said Myrtle sweetly, her face blushing slightly.

'Come on you,' I pulled her briskly away from the Trickle doorstep. 'We've still got work to do, Bugface!' There was no time to waste. The plan needed to be put into action.

The pilp plant was only on the other side of school so we wouldn't be too long, after all, I still had the nightsgritch to do. Perhaps the light would appear – oh blast, the pictures! With all the fuss about Gilbert I'd completely forgotten about them. I really needed Fred to see them.

'Fred, the pictures, you didn't look at them. I need you to have a look only I think I can just make out some ...'

'Well, we kind of had other things going on, didn't we?' Fred interrupted. 'I'll look at them later when I've more time.'

'But Fred, I think there may be a picture of ...' I tried to reason with him but he was hell bent on getting to the pilp plant to check out the Cruet contract.

'Why don't you check the pictures out further ... and meet up with us later?' he suggested.

'What on my own?' I called but he had already gone.

Clutching Gilbert to his chest he turned the corner sharply and headed towards the pilp plant. Bessie followed closely while Myrtle flew just behind.

'Myrtle, you coming?' I called after her.

'No. I can't. They might need me to get Gilbert back in the jar,' Myrtle replied awkwardly. She shrugged her shoulders and hurried to catch up.

'Suit yourself, Bugface!' I said. 'I'll go on my own then.'

Okay, I would concentrate on the pictures. I had to find something to make them look clearer, something more powerful than my enlarger but where would I find anything like that? Of course, it was so obvious – school!

Chapter Ten

The school wasn't that far from Fred's house. Slight problem though – it would be locked up at this time. My only hope was the window. There was one at the back of the hall that was always hard to shut. If I could get through there, then all I had to do was avoid setting off the Grublin keeperouter alarm.

I made my way round to the back where the hall was and headed straight to where I expected to get in. Blast, the window was tight shut. Mr Scurge, the takecarer, must have fixed it – typical. There had to be some way in surely, a small window or door – or door! Brilliant, the side entrance was slightly ajar.

Tscchh – just wide enough for me to squeeze through. A quick look round just to make sure the coast was clear and I was in. The door led onto the corridor where the classchambers were based. The science lab was at the far end. That was where the most powerful and even larger enlargers were kept.

I crawled low along the corridor, past the long line of portraits of former heads; *Mr Krusp – thirty seven days – died in office – literally, Mrs Hirch – twenty three days service – scared to death by Grublins* ... the list went on and on. They looked down mockingly.

So far, so good. I'd passed my classchamber, no alarm bells. Still a way to go though to reach the lab and the worst bit was yet to come – Fettock's office. I knew the school was empty but the thought of crawling past his room filled me with dread. It all felt so eerie, so quiet and so very cold.

All I had to do was keep my head down and press forward. Concentrate on the enlarger, think about the pictures ... and worry about the light.

What was that?

Scrinch, Scrunch, Scrinch, Scrunch

Footsteps – oh no! – and nowhere to hide. This could only mean one thing.

'Rather late to be in school, Lichen, wouldn't you say?'

'A-A-Ah, Mr Fettock. Well, it was just that ...' I had to quickly think of something – 'it was just that ... I lost one of my earrings, special they were, a present from my Gran.'

I stood up quickly, feeling a little stupid having crawled most of the way down the corridor. But the strap of my bag had got itself twisted around my leg and in my hurry to get up the bag of pictures tumbled to the ground. They fell out, sliding across the freshly polished floor for all to see. I tried frantically to gather them back up but it was too late, Fettock already had two in his hands.

'What's all this then, Lichen, hey?' he asked, glaring at me. 'You'd better come into my office and explain yourself before I ... before I ... send a dragonfly to your mother.' His voice tailed off as he stared at the pictures. He sat down in his oversized chair, his eyes not leaving his spoils.

'I-I-I can explain,' I stuttered, 'I just wanted to look at the pictures under the enlarger.'

'Why couldn't you just wait until tomorrow like any normal fairy?' He turned the pictures round and round in his hand.

'I was just impatient, I wanted to see if they revealed anything more about ... *you know.*' I kind of mumbled the last few words hoping he'd ignore it.

'Revealed more about – *you know*?' He looked up, his brow furrowed. 'Is that some kind of code, Lichen? What is – *you know*?'

'*The light,* Mr Fettock.' Again I mumbled hoping he would lose interest but again, no!

'Oh *the light*! Oh, I shouldn't worry about that, Lichen. It turned out to be nothing but a very angry firefly.' He leant back heavily, his chair chipping the enamel as it hit the wall. 'Arty Granger apparently 'bumped' into it last nightsgritch and ended up with a badly burnt leg.'

Arty Granger? But he never went on nightsgritches, not ever.

'I'm surprised you didn't know, especially as it was your brother Albert who told me about it.'

Albert?

'I must say I was pleased to see an end to all the

mystery that surrounded that light. At least if it happens again we'll know why.'

The light was a firefly? I'd seen it first hand. I knew that was rubbish. I couldn't believe he would think that was true. No way was that a firefly.

'So now what should I do with you, Lichen? Breaking and entering, huh?'

'Well, it was more entering really, no actual breaking took place at all, honestly, Mr Fettock, sir.'

'Well, I suppose no harm was done but in future, Lichen, enter the school through the front door and only during school hours, right?' He gestured towards the door.

'I don't suppose I could still borrow the enlarger?'

'Out Lichen, before I send that dragonfly!'

'What about my pictures, the ones in your hand?'

'I said out, Lichen! Consider the pictures ... confiscated.' And with that he shut the office door firmly behind me.

I made a swift exit worried that he might change his mind about the dragonfly. What I couldn't understand though was why he didn't want to take the matter further. It was just so not like him – and he'd kept my pictures!

****

I left the school feeling more than a little stupid and annoyed with myself, and flew across to the pilp plant to meet the rest of the gang. I was a little curious to know what had happened in my absence. I didn't have to wait long to find out. The large crowd of fairies, some holding their noses, some with scarves over their faces, was a sure fact that Gilbert had been let loose. A revolting smell oozed from each of the large mirrored windows and slithered snake-like under the doors into the road. Then it – he – wafted mischievously under the noses of unsuspecting fairies, before returning to the building itself. Mr Cruet stood in the middle of the road comforting some of his clients, the ones with a lot of credits naturally.

As I flew in nearer, I could just make out the figures of Ma and Pa, faces covered by their hands, trying to talk to another fairy. Ma was obviously having problems making her self understood so was swapping between removing her hand from her mouth and talking then, when she could stand the smell no more, returning her hand to her face. Pa, sensibly, just kept his hand where it was.

I flew around the other side of the building, anxious not to be spotted by either of them. Inside I could hear the pilp grinding machine crashing away noisily and the screech of the extractor as it removed the silver scrigger. But above all this noise there was an even worse racket to be heard – Fred and Myrtle were arguing furiously.

'Well, you try if you're so clever!' Myrtle screamed. I pressed my nose up close to the window to get a better look. I could see a really cross Myrtle thrusting a jar and its lid into the stomach of an even more cross Fred. She stomped across the floor and sat on the pilp extractor pipe.

'We'd have got him first time if you did as I said,' Fred screamed back.

'Oh yeah, like I'd agree to go the pilpblast with a smell like him.'

'Well, you could have just pretended, you know, just a little white lie.' He lowered his voice and walked towards her, shoving the jar angrily back at her.

'I'm not lying, Fred, no way.' She pushed the jar back at Fred once more and headed towards the door, 'Oh, I'm going home. I'm fed up with all this,'

As they continued to yell at each other, Gilbert, alias the greeny-yellow wisp, was weaving in and out of them, stirring things up. He was obviously enjoying his smelly self. It was great viewing. Fairies would pay good credits to see entertainment like that. He was winding them both up beautifully. But I had to act fast, Myrtle was leaving and Gilbert was still loose. I swooped in through the back door.

'Oi! Stop messing around you two, time's running out,' I shouted, 'Cruet will suspect something soon and Ma and Pa are out there, Myrtle. – Now where's Bessie got to?'

'I'm here, Aggie,' Bessie called from the office. 'I was just looking at the contract on Cruet's desk. It seems ...'

I had to interrupt urgently, 'Bess, we haven't got time for that now, we need to get out ...' The main door creaked noisily as it slowly began to open. 'Quick! Now threaten Gilbert or we'll all be caught.'

Bessie did her 'you know that I know and I'll tell everyone if you don't get in the jar' trick ... Snap! ... and Gilbert was contained once again.

'Phew! That was too close for comfort,' I said as we emerged from the back exit. Myrtle and Fred exchanged dirty looks and sulked quietly. Bessie however, was eager to share what she'd found out and flew up to join me.

'It's all true, Aggie. Cruet does indeed have a right to sell the pilp plant as his family have run it for the last one hundred years ...' she began, flicking her plaits behind her shoulders.

'Marvellous, so we're all going to be at the mercy of Arty Granger. He's going to grow rich on our pilp credits and yet he's never done a single nightsgritch in his life.'

'I haven't finished yet. There was a small clause that Cruet seemed to have conveniently forgotten to mention.' Bessie hesitated, preparing herself for a big finish as we turned the corner.

Fred began to unsulk and was now listening hard to what Bessie was saying.

'The contract states that a buyer must be found within thirty days from the one hundredth anniversary otherwise – and this is the good bit – ownership is handed back to Pilpsville Council for the next one hundred years, then it can be sold again if it's stayed in the same hands – blah, blah, blah.' Bessie grinned broadly.

'So we just need to put off the buyer until the thirtieth day has passed,' said Fred, rubbing his crown tuft thoughtfully.

'Yes, that's right,' said Bessie, still managing to grin broadly while talking.

'And how do you suppose we're going to do that, huh?' I asked.

'Oh, I don't know but I'm sure we'll think of something,' Bessie replied, incredibly still grinning madly.

'Bessie, I don't mean to be rude but have you got a dragonfly wing stuck in your mouth or something?'

'No, it's just that your Ma is heading this way and I'm giving her the impression that we're happy to see her and that we haven't really been snooping around in the pilp plant!'

Huge grins all round now. Even Myrtle took time out from her sulking to grin widely at Ma.

'You've been up to something, haven't you?' said Ma, flying in to meet us.

'What's in that jar, Bessie? It doesn't look very nice.'

'Umm, I-I'm just taking him – it – home, actually. I'd best go, mum waiting and that.'

'Yeah, me too – home to go to – nightsgritch to get ready for ...' Fred's voice trailed off as he fled from Ma's gaze to follow Bessie's quick exit.

'Hmmm,' said Ma, giving me a look. 'You've been up to something – I can tell!'

She grabbed Bugface's hand and flew off in the direction of home. I followed, my head spinning madly. Thirty days seemed like a long time but was it enough time?

Chapter Eleven

On arriving home, Ma delivered a long, long lecture to Bugface and me on the perils of hanging around the pilp plant with so much machinery to get mangled in.

'... and those grinders could mash your brain to a pulp – that is of course if you both still had one!'

It was the same lecture I had heard regularly for the past ten years, so the fear had worn off a while ago. Still I was polite enough to acknowledge that certain dangers were still there – in the form of Mr Cruet, not that I told Ma that.

For dinner, Ma had made a scurtch and gibberd casserole which was eaten in relative silence as she felt a little reflective thinking was in order!

'Hell, that was painful,' I said, winking at Myrtle as we returned to the bedroom.

'Blimey, all that fuss over nothing. If only she knew ...' Myrtle pretended to mop her brow.

'Well, she doesn't know, and not so much of the blimey, miss!'

Myrtle giggled. 'Do I really have to stay here, Aggie? Can't I come with you and Bessie on the nightsgritch?'

'No, you can't, young fairy.' Ma put her head round the door. 'Flapstopping practise in the garden, now!'

'Oh, Ma!' Myrtle stomped noisily out of the room and into the garden. I stood for a minute watching her 'fall' dramatically from the top of the wooden flapstop pole. It was hilarious. She would act out a little routine then tumble from the pole. Luckily the small green net cushioned her fall each time.

'Are you off now?' Pa called from the kitchen.

'Yeah, but where are the pilp sacks?'

'They should be tucked under the acorn shelf.'

There was one tatty pilp sack stuck in the corner. It would have to do.

I shouted my goodbyes and made my way to meet Bessie. She was sitting on the front step of her house waiting patiently for me.

'How's your mum now? Has she calmed down a bit?' she asked as we flew down towards the crossing.

'Yeah, she's fine. I just need to make sure I collect a good few pilps tonight if I'm going to keep her sweet.'

'Oh, I nearly forgot, Fred said he'll try to meet up with us later. It depends on if he can find a suitable place to store Gilbert.'

As we spoke we could see the portal at the crossing open and swooped down to pass through. I began to feel very confident that this would be a great night for pilp collecting. It was a beautiful evening and the bright, sparkly stars followed me and Bessie closely as we flew to our usual collecting patch. We happily tossed one pilp after the other into our sacks, chatting casually as we went.

But the peace and quiet of the evening was quickly shattered as we arrived outside the blue house with the windmill. Bessie stopped in her tracks and pointed at the two shady figures, hovering outside an upstairs window. The short dumpy one crashed noisily into the stone window sill, catching her leg on the broken plaster and letting out a howl in pain. A third one was shouting instructions from a nearby branch.

'Hey, Aggie', shouted Bessie. 'Look who's collecting in our area again.'

Oh great! It was Gertie Cruet with her faithful followers.

They immediately flew over and began to hover irritatingly around us.

'Had a good night, have you?' said Petunia, eyeing us up and down.

'Collected enough for your dress yet?' Violet's words stung viciously.

'We're doing just fine so why don't you all just push off and find your own,' I shouted.

Gertie Cruet flew down from the branch to join them. She dived down beneath me. I felt quite relieved that she had at last heeded my words. But she was again to have the last laugh.

A shout came from below me. 'But why should we leave when it's such easy pickings here. I mean, it doesn't rain pilps every nightsgritch does it?' Gertie put her hand over her mouth and sniggered.

She must have been at her father's berry wine because she was making no sense at all.

'I haven't got time for this, Gertie. Just leave us be. We need to get finished.'

'Oh you've started already then, have you? Looking at your sack, no one would think so!' Then she sniggered again, this time more loudly and was joined by her cronies. She pointed at the sack I was carrying on my back. 'Honestly, Lichen, you're such a loser.'

'She's right, Aggie. Look at your sack,' Bessie said.

'Oh don't you start Bess. You're supposed to be my friend,' I growled.

The sack came off my back quite easily, a little surprising as we'd been collecting for the past two hours.

Damn! It was empty. The hole in the corner of the bag confirmed Gertie's 'raining pilps' theory. The anxious look on my face was all that Gertie needed to satisfy her cruel nature.

'Come on, you two, let's go and see if there are any pilp puddles lower down,' she cackled loudly, dragging Violet and Petunia further downwards. Their laughter echoed as they moved further away.

'Flipping heck, Bess. I don't believe this, not

again,' my voice began to falter.

'Come on, Aggie. It's not your fault. How were you to know that there was a hole in the sack when you picked it up?'

Albert! He must have left that damaged sack in the hallway the other nightsgritch and I'd picked it up.

'It was Albert's sack,' I mumbled. 'He came home with one like that the other night.'

'Never mind, Aggie, we've still got a bit more time. Come on, let's move on to the big house with the red door, that's always good for collecting.'

And so we flew on, silently making our way to the big house with the red door.

We worked quickly and quietly for the next few hours. I wasn't in the mood for talking although Bessie tried her hardest to cheer me up with a sorry string of really bad jokes. Then we got onto the subject of Phyllis and the light.

'Have you looked at her closely, Bess? I mean really closely,' I asked.

'I can't say I have,' said Bessie, 'I mean she's not that close a friend. Why d'you ask?'

'Well, it's just that she looked a little – grey. Didn't you notice when we were at the meeting?'

'Not really, I mean she had that scarf wrapped round her face most of the evening. But saying that, I did notice her eyes. They were really, hmm, bulgy like – and red, from crying I expect.'

'And her speech, Bess, have you noticed that? It seems a bit strange too.'

'Well, it's not surprising she's so under the weather when you think of all she's gone through lately, is it?'

I was sure there was more to Phyllis than just being 'under the weather'. My thinking face seemed to give Bessie cause for alarm. She thought I was still sulking but my ears had pricked up at a strange sound.

'Come on, Aggie, it's not so bad. We've done all right considering ...'

'Sssshhh!'

'Don't be so rude. I was just saying ...'

'Ssshhh.'

'If you tell me to ssshhh once more ...'

'Ssshhh. Listen – what was that, Bess? I'm sure I heard something.' Perhaps it was the light.

Then I heard it again, only this time getting closer. I tugged sharply at Bessie's wings causing her to turn suddenly.

'Come on Bess, this way – something's not right.'

We dived down between the grove of great nash trees that lay at back of the house with the blue door. The gentle breeze suddenly broke into a strong fierce wind. It howled loudly through the branches. We landed quickly, grabbing the nearest branch and holding tightly as the tree shook violently from the sudden onslaught. I pricked up my ears once more, only this time the noise the wind was making completely camouflaged any other sound.

'There's nothing out there, Aggie. It's just the wind.'

'No, Bessie, there was definitely something. I'd lay credits on it.' My sixth sense was now hard at work, my wings acting as aerials, trying to pick up a signal. Something was most definitely out there.

The wind continued to rant and rage angrily at everything in its path, including us. I spotted a piece of string attached to a deflated balloon and tied it around my waist, throwing the remainder at a stump near to the tree's trunk.

Using the string as our guide we somehow managed to crawl along the branch throwing ourselves into an old disused squirrel's hole. After giving each other a brush down and shaking the wind out of our wings, we gingerly stepped towards the front of the hole.

'This is just *so* wrong, Bessie. One minute the weather's fine and the next it's like a flipping hurricane.'

And then, just as it started, the wind suddenly stopped.

'There, I told you,' said Bessie. 'It was just a fluke wind, nothing to worry ...' she paused, turning her ears to the left, then to the right. Her eyes opening widely, now expressed a startled and anxious look.

'Can you hear that, Aggie? Can you?' she asked worriedly, the confident, assured look rapidly disappearing from her face as she spoke. 'Grublins! Oh no, it's Grublins, Aggie. They've sniffed us out! What'll we do?'

'No Bess, not Grublins – listen!'

As I watched the colour drain from Bessie's face I realised my suspicions were well founded. There was no mistaking it now. The noise had returned.

The first indicator was a faint tinkling sound. Not so bad you may think but after several minutes, as the noise got closer and closer, the tinkling changed to a horrific crashing. Even the burds ran scared at this, followed by all manner of tree dwelling creatures fleeing to the lower branches. The crashing continued, becoming louder by the second but now it was being persistently interrupted by a high pitched screeching – which we now knew to our cost, would be followed by a glittering trail of sparks! Bessie and I froze to the spot. We stared numbly at each other as the truth suddenly dawned on us – SPRITES!

Now we really *were* in trouble. Sprites – green, flying, mischievous creatures with large floppy ears, large non-blinking eyes and even larger mouths. Their shrill screaming broke windows, bottles, doors, in fact anything that was made of glass, – including jars containing putrid smelling former fairies!

'Quick Bess, we've got to get to the exit before they catch up with us. If they get through to Pilpsville again all hell will break loose.'

'Yeah, remember what happened last time,' she said breathlessly.

As we reached the exit, the tinkling and screeching had alerted many other collectors. Several older fairies were stretching a large orange net in front of the door to catch them in. It was our first line of defence. After that they only had to open the door and they would be through. Other fairies were ushering in-coming collectors through to the other side.

'Quickly,' cried the fairy usher, pushing a younger fairy through, 'and when you get there, tell them we need reinforcements urgently if we're to hold the door.'

There was little Bessie and I could do but return home. I'd managed to collect about half a sackful, using a pin to hold the bottom of the sack together. I'd explain what had happened to Ma and then I'd have a few choice words to share with Albert. Stupid, was good for a start followed by idiot, irresponsible and selfish.

We joined the panicking crowd desperately trying to exit and escape the inevitable onslaught.

'Poke your elbows out, Bessie and push or we'll never get out. Bessie? Bessie?' I turned to see where she was. I'd lost her somehow in the crowd, which was now pushing harder and harder as the crashing and screeching got nearer and nearer. Hands started grabbing at faces to remove spectacles in, surely, a wasted effort to keep them from cracking. And still the noise got louder.

'Bessie, where are you?' I cried, trying to claw my way backwards through the panicking crowd.

'Oi, watch it,' an irate fairy called as I stepped on his foot in my hurry to get past.

'S-Sorry, I just need to find my friend.'

'Look where you're going,' came an angry shout as I caught another's wing.

'S-Sorry, sorry.'

Gradually, with much heaving, pushing and shoving, I found my way to the back of the crowd to where I hoped I might find Bessie. But there was no sign of her anywhere and the noise was almost on top of us now. The vast majority of fairies had now passed through the exit while the remaining few were holding the net up high and wide ready to catch the sprites before they made their latest attempt to storm Pilpsville.

'Flipping sprites,' mumbled one net holder. 'Always after our magic dust.'

'Yeah,' agreed another, 'just so that they can sneak it under the donors' pillow and wish for what *they* want.'

They were right. It made our pilp collections so much harder, not to mention the donors' disappointment. I mean ten gallons of plom beer wasn't really what your average pilp donor expected to find under their pillow when they woke up.

But where was Bessie in all this? I couldn't see her anywhere. What I could see was a huge green mass heading directly at me, screeching loudly and, in the distance, the golden remains of a burnt out trail. The sprites were here and in full force by the look of it. I had no choice but to grab hold of the net and stand firm with the others to try and keep the invaders at bay until the cavalry arrived!

I managed to fold down my ears just as the sprites poured down on top of us in the hope that they would filter out some of the dreadful noises they were making.

They flew around mockingly, cursing us in spritespiel, flapping their hideously oversized ears to spread the sound further. The noise was alarming and fairies started to succumb to its shrill tone, losing their grip on the net, holding their ears and crumbling into heaps on the ground. It was terrifying! But I had to hold fast.

'mfu ju hp!' screamed one of the sprites into my face – whatever that meant.

'And back at you, matey,' I screamed back, still clinging desperately to my piece of net. But there were too many of them and the reinforcements had still not arrived. They screamed louder and flew lower and lower until they found a gap in the net – a gap where a fairy should have been holding it. The fairy concerned was tightly curled up on the ground, rolling from side to side, holding his ears.

'uijt xbz – b ipmf,' shouted the leading sprite, pointing to the gap in the net. The green mass stopped and the unblinking eyes turned and stared. In a matter of seconds there was a mad dash as they scrambled to get through, jostling and heaving each other out of the way in their efforts to be first. There was one thing they hadn't thought of though, the exit door, it was still closed. I threw myself towards it, spreading my arms and legs across it, barring their way. Oh heck, what *was* I thinking of?

A large and extremely ugly green sprite loomed down on me. 'npwf, qjmq dpmmfdups!' it growled. Its grotesque face was distorted with rage, its huge mouth dripped with saliva and its breath smelt of dirty socks.

'I don't know what you're on about but no way am I letting you through,' I shouted back bravely.

'Don't lean too hard on that bar, Aggie, it'll open up.' Bessie appeared from behind a tree, rubbing her head vigorously.

'Bessie! Are you all right? – Sorry, what did you say? I can hardly hear anything above this din.'

'I said, don't lean to hard on the door, Aggie, or the bar will ...'

Too late! In my efforts to keep them from opening the door I, myself, had kindly opened it for them by pushing down on the exit bar. They scurried through, thrusting me to one side and I think one actually had the nerve to say thank you as it went past.

A 'supposed to be holding the net' fairy pulled himself up from the ground and looked at me in disgust. 'Oh, that's just marvellous, Aggie. You've let them in.'

'Excuse me! Wasn't I the one holding the net, defending the honour of the door etc, etc!'

'Take no notice, Aggie. I'm sure you did all you could,' said Bessie, rubbing her forehead where a large purple bruise had started to appear.

'You mean you didn't actually see, Bess? Great, now everyone's going to think that I did it on purpose. You were my only hope.'

'Sorry, but I must have been out cold for quite a while. I don't know what happened. One minute you were next to me, then there was a noise and I turned round and this strange buzzy sounding light was in the trees behind me. Then I must have fell and banged my head.'

'You must have whacked your head really hard, Bess. Green, screeching mass was what you saw, remember?' I pulled a face that I thought resembled a sprite. 'Like this but green and screechy.'

'No, that's NOT what I saw! I told you – buzzy, yellowy, hovering light thingy.'

'Sorry, run that by me again!'

'Angry fly sound, Buzzzzzz buzzzzz ?'

Ah ha! *The light*! Great timing. The sprites invasion of Pilpsville was under way and it had decided to appear now, marvellous!

'So where'd you see it?'

'I told you ...'

'Exactly, where?' I interrupted sharply.

Bessie pointed to a tree in the distance, which tree was anyfairy's guess.

'Can you take me to it, Bess? Only I can't quite decide if you mean the green and brown one there or the other green and brown one there!!'

'Oh, do I have to? My head hurts. Can't we look another time? Sprite invasion underway ...'

'Oh, come on, Bess. Why hurry back now, and anyway, you've seen *the light* – so to speak.'

'But everyone will be wondering where we are, and what if the sprites get to my house?'

'Bess, this is our only real chance to discover who or what the light is – please! We can listen to what's happening through the sixth sense aerial.' I twisted the tip of my wing to pick up a signal.

'All right, all right, but it'll have to be quick. The sun will be up in less than an hour.'

'Great, you won't regret it, Bessie.'

'Yeah, but you might!'

Chapter Twelve

It took a while to try to find the tree where Bessie saw the light, mainly because she kept back tracking to have another look from a different angle – probably to do with that bang on the head.

'Ah, *get off me you great green brute and leave me geraniums alone!*'

CRASH! *'You little devil. That was my best beer glass!'*

'If my Wilbert was here now he'd ...' SMASH!

'Turn the aerial down, Aggie. It's making my headache worse.' Bessie held her head once more. It looked like it had all been a wasted effort. It was time to admit defeat and head home. But in the time it took to turn around, it – the light – reappeared in a small clearing, on the lower branch of a small berrch tree. There was no buzz or movement from it. Perhaps Albert was right, perhaps it was just an angry firefly, although it seemed to have calmed down a lot now.

'Right, let's creep up nice and slowly,' I whispered.

'Okay.'

'No sudden movements, yeah?'

'Okay!'

'And no talking.'

'AAAHHH, it's got me dragonfly. Gerroff! Poor Percy can't carry your weight!'

'Okay!! Okay!! I'm not stupid, you know!' Bessie's voice became louder with each indignant word.

'Ear plugs for sale! Only one hundred credits.'

'Ssssshhhh! You'll frighten it away,' Bessie said sarcastically, then pointed to my wing tip.

Flying as silently as possible, aerial turned down to its lowest level, we flew from tree to tree, inching our way closer with each flap. The light remained on the branch.

'My head aches. Can we stop for a minute?' Bessie whispered from behind a tree. She was holding her head where a large purple lump was protruding.

'Oh but Bess, I've been waiting for this for ages. It might move on if we're not quick.'

'Well, you go on. I'll wait here for a bit.' Bessie settled on a nearby branch. 'I can listen to the sprite invasion on my own aerial while you're gone.'

'If you're sure. You can catch me up when you're ready.' I didn't need to be told twice. I was off, this was my chance. I would be hailed a hero – heroine.

I flew gently behind the next tree, I was so near. Just a little further, just a little nearer and I should be able to identify what or who the light was. I began to feel a little sick with excitement and my heart was beating so hard I thought it would surely be heard and give me away. Just a few branches to scramble through then hover behind a few leaves so as not to be seen. Wow! There it was in all it's glory, but it had its back to me, damn. Bright and yellowy-white, it seemed as tall as a fairy and it had wings. If it was a firefly, it was rather big. I hovered a little closer, landing and pulling a few bleech leaves in front of my face, leaving just enough room for my eyes to see out. I could just make out something projecting from its back, a long shape sort of like a tube – no wait, there were two tube shapes – they seemed to be joined together. They reminded me of something I'd seen before somewhere – but where? Something of a similar shape, joined in that way, two tubes strapped together.

Oh, no ... please no. It can't be ... no. I must be mistaken.

The leaves crashed together as I let go of them in disbelief, the noise of which made *it* flinch and quickly fly off. By the time I had gathered my senses, all six of them, *it* had disappeared altogether. I had to stop and sit. I had to think this through ...

'Oh, there you are. I've been looking for you for ages.' Bessie had recovered enough to catch me up. 'What's the matter? You've got a face like a wet nightsgritch. Didn't you find it after all?'

Oh, if only you knew, Bessie, I thought to myself.

Her sixth sense aerial continued to blast out invasion updates.

'You give me that back you slimy green slurg.'

'How's your head?' I had to change the conversation quickly. 'Feeling better are you?'

'Aggie! What about the light? Did you find it? Aggie?'

What Bessie had said earlier about me regretting following the light played on my mind. I wondered if she knew how much it rang true. But how could I tell her? How could I tell anyone?

'Blast! They're everywhere! I've got to find somewhere safe for this jar.'

'Oh, hell. That's Fred's voice, Aggie. We've got to go – NOW!'

****

The sun was just about to show its face as we neared the exit. The ground in front of the door was still littered with bits of net and a few odd pieces of clothing that had been left behind during all the commotion. The door itself was scratched and dented from the initial attack. In all other respects the exit was as you'd expect at this time, closed, empty and quiet. Unfortunately that was not the case on the other side of the door!

'Pigging hell!!' Bessie gasped, mouth dropping open, eyes bulging and head banging.

And it certainly looked as if hell had come to town. Small, green, unwelcome, objects were swooping and dive bombing everywhere – sprites. A chilling mixture of screeching and screaming filled the air. On the ground, tiny slithers of glass from windows formed glittering carpets. And flying desperately in and out of their houses were the rudely awakened fairy folk of Incisorton. Many were clutching sacred glassware of some sentimental value. It made them easy targets for the sprites who had sensed what they were up to. *Crash!* Another vase hit the ground as the owner tried desperately to cover his ears. The sprites squealed with delight and moved onto to the next victim, cracking the glass in her spectacles. As we flew nearer to the centre of town, the scene was much the same, screeching and screaming followed by the incessant sound of breaking glass.

'Quickly, Aggie. Let's cut round the back to Fred's.'

Bessie was still holding her head and looked kind of pale. 'I hope they've managed to transfer Gilbert from that glass jar to another container.'

'Yeah, whatever.' The last thing I needed was to see Fred. He most likely had his suspicions as to the identity of *it*. He'd seen the pictures – he probably knew and wasn't saying. What if he and Fettock suspected? But what if they didn't know – they still had evidence. I needed it. I needed to get back those pictures from Fettock and the picture negatives from Fred's. At least with those gone there would be no evidence, no suspicions as to who the light or 'it' was.

'Yeah, Fred's house,' I said, 'after all we don't want Gilbert to get loose again, do we?'

No, that would be ... brilliant! Yes! He would make the perfect cover as I searched Fred's house for the pictures.

But getting to Fred's house was going to prove more difficult than we had expected for there, blocking our way, was a swarm of sprites. Some were hanging from washing lines, trying on the clothing in the process. Others were chasing pyjama clad young fairies or trying to catch their pet dragonflies who had been allowed out for exercise. And there in the middle of the chaos stood two sprites, both very green but one easily larger and uglier than the other. They were punching and kicking each other relentlessly whilst screaming or possibly cursing in spritespiel. The smaller one was pointing towards the crossing and trying to pull the larger one in that direction. The larger one was having none of that and pulled at the smaller ones nose. That little gesture seemed to make it lose the plot completely and it reached for an empty dustbin, swinging it round and round before landing it straight in the big one's stomach

Sprites now started to gather round in force to watch the two battle it out.

'Quick, Aggie ... this is our chance ... this is our chance ... to get by without being noticed ...'

Bessie grabbed my arm and started to pull me in the direction of Fred's house. My eyes were still firmly glued to the intriguing sight of two sprites knocking all hell out of each other in the middle of our town, surrounded by a heaving green mass of supporters. So much for the invasion.

'Please, Aggie, I'm starting to feel a little ... a little ...' her grip on my arm loosened as she started to flutter slowly downwards.

'Bessie!' I screamed.

She'd fainted. I dropped quickly beneath her, grabbing at her lifeless body as she headed towards the ground. She was out cold. Using all the strength I could muster, I managed to pull her back upwards and started to haul her along to Fred's. But soon my arms began to feel heavy and ached from the extra weight. How much further could I go like this?

I struggled on albeit at a slow pace, aware of the sprite danger that could appear at any moment. Suddenly the load felt lighter. I could feel the blood start to flow back into my arms. Another fairy had swept under the other side of Bessie's limp body. I had never been so pleased to see Myrtle in my life.

'What happened to her, Aggie?'

I explained briefly – hole in sack – Gertie Cruet – sprites – door opening – bang on head.

Of course I didn't mention anything about *it*. That was a burden I had to carry not poor Myrtle.

'We should take her home really,' I said, focusing back onto the present, 'but I don't know if we can get through. We thought it was quicker to get to Fred's. Now I just want to get her home to her mum.'

Bessie started to come round and wiped the dribble from the corner of her mouth as she tried to talk.

'Go to Fred's, Aggie … it's nearer … send a dragonfly to my mum.' She sunk down heavily again although with the load shared it was easier to bear this time.

'Fred's then,' Myrtle nodded in agreement.

We flew quickly and quietly, keeping to the trees to avoid any encounters with sprites but most still seemed to be preoccupied with the scrap we'd left behind. Dotted about were a few stragglers pulling up plants, running across roofs and generally making a nuisance of themselves. And all the time the high pitched screeching went on relentlessly. We managed to pull Bessie's ears down a little in an effort to shield her from the din.

'Good grief, why must they do that? How comes they don't go deaf with all that racket?' Myrtle muttered quietly under her breath so as not to draw attention to us.

'Don't know, don't care!' I snapped, exhausted by the extra weight of Bessie. 'Let's just get to Fred's before we're seen.'

We had nearly reached his front gate when something sharp hit my arm from behind.

'Just keep going Myrtle. Don't look round.' It was becoming a little scary now. Where was Fred? Why wasn't he watching out for us?

Ouch! Something else had caught the back of my neck. Then Myrtle squealed as a plant pot smacked her hard on the leg.

'Ow! Aggie, they've seen us. What shall we do?' she sobbed. Her eyes were full of fear and alarm.

'Duck down, Myrtle,' I screamed as another flying object soared over her head.

'Aggie, I'm scared.' She was becoming hysterical now.

Well that did it. Making my little sister cry like that, throwing things at her, scaring her, well no more. I was considerably hacked off.

'Go through the gate and knock at the door, Myrtle,' I shouted. 'Tell Fred to get Gilbert.'

I propped Bessie up against the fence as yet another object hit me, this time on the back. I pretended to ignore them as I boldly fished around in the bottom of Bessie's pilp sack and slipped off my belt.

'Now you're for it!' I turned around smartly, catapult and ammunition ready in hand, the look of a maniac on my face.

Boing!

Smack! Sprite number one fell from the branch where it'd been firing things from. 'px!' it yelled, clutching his head.

Boing!

WHACK! Sprite number two rolled on the ground, thumping it with its fists, rubbing its bottom – and crying it would seem!

I was on a roll now! Take that!

Boing!

CRACK! Oops, that was a window. So sorry!

After several rounds the catapult had claimed a good few victims, leaving the ground littered with sprites clutching at some part of their hideous bodies.

Boing!

THUMP! Another one hit the ground.

'... and that one's for Myrtle!' I shouted as one fell from the tree opposite me.

They rolled on the ground, wriggling and writhing in agony, holding various bruised and battered limbs and other body parts. In a strange way I felt a bit sorry for them but then I remembered the havoc they had caused and how they had made my sister cry. I had one pilp left. I loaded the belt – catapult – and swung round for a final assault.

Where'd they gone? I let the belt catapult drop to the ground. A loud shrieking noise overhead made me look up. There in the sky was a huge green gathering of sprites, including several whimpering ones. It looked like they had finished messing around and were ready to take what they'd come for, the fairy – magic – dust.

Myrtle came running out of Fred's and threw her arms around my neck.

'That was brilliant, Aggie,' she cried.

Fred came running out of the front door. 'Well done, you soon scared them off. I'd have helped but what with transferring Gilbert to a plastic bottle and trying to stop the sprites coming down the chimney, I was a little busy.'

'No worries. Now quick, help me get Bessie inside,' I said, slipping my arm around Bessie's waist carefully.

'We can put her in mum's room. Give us a hand, Myrtle!' said Fred.

Between the three of us we managed to haul the limp body of Bessie inside the house and into the bedroom. We covered her up gently and headed back outside.

'Now what about Gilbert, have you got him? Only it looks like they've all headed for the pilp plant.'

'I've got him here.' Fred patted his trouser pocket.

'Might be best if I take him. I may be able to get a better shot with my belt.'

'I'm sorry but do you mean to shoot my little brother into the midst of a heaving mass of ugly, screeching, havoc reeking sprites?' Fred asked indignantly.

'Well, yeah. That was the plan.'

'Oh, okay then!' He casually threw Gilbert to me and I put him safely in my sack.

'What about me, Aggie?'

I'd forgotten about Myrtle. She was waiting at the gate.

'Might be best if you stayed here,' I said.

'But why can't I come?' she whined.

'Because it's too dangerous. You know, sprites – scary, screechy creatures.' I made a spritelike move in an effort to convince her.

'But I could help ...'

I was running out of time and patience. 'Fred!' I shouted, and nodded at Bugface.

I watched as he reasoned with her.

' ... and besides Bessie will want a friendly face there when she wakes up, won't she?'

'Yeah, I suppose so.' She crossed her arms, her bottom lip protruding sulkily and made her way to the front door.

' … and remember to listen out for Bessie's mum,' I called after her.

'Right,' said Fred, 'let's do it! Let's smell 'em out.'

We flew off speedily, cutting in and out of anywhere that would put us some distance ahead of the sprites. All around was a scene of utter devastation. Broken pots and shattered glasses covered the ground. Splinters of glass hung precariously from cracked windows. But the worst was yet to come. Fred let out a gasp of despair.

'Oh no, Aggie. Look what they've done to the fountain of eternal tooth!'

The fountain, made from ancient pilp, had been smashed beyond recognition. Its silver scrigger pipe work twisted and contorted into strange yet amusing shapes.

'Don't you think that bit looks like a dragonfly, Fred?' I said, pointing at one particular piece of scrigger.

He gave me a look.

'I'm sorry but you know I don't believe in all that nonsense.'

'That's not the point,' he said. 'We need to put a stop to all this now. Let's cut through decay alley. That should put us ahead.'

Thankfully sprites weren't the best or most accurate fliers and as we approached the pilp plant they had yet to appear.

'Get Gilbert ready, Aggie, but don't unscrew the top just yet.'

I lifted the sack off my back and rummaged around at the bottom. Now where was it?

'Come on, Aggie. Don't mess about. We need to be ready.'

I dug around a little more, looking desperately for the bottle. Unfortunately the only thing I could see was the gaping hole. I'd lost Gilbert!

'Aggie, I can hear them, come on, get Gilbert out.'

'I-I-I-I can't seem to ...'

My answer was interrupted by a familiar and highly irritating cackle.

'Lost something, Lichen?' Gertie Cruet was perched on the pilp plant roof, waving a bottle around in the air – Gilbert!

'Yeah, she seems to have 'lost her bottle' again,' sneered Petunia and Violet together, sitting on the chimney stack behind.

Oh great! The sprites were approaching fast and Gertie had the only real weapon we could use to send them packing.

The screeching grew louder and louder, making the inhabitants of nearby houses emerge from their homes. News of the sprite invasion was about to reach them head on. Mr Wriddle, the pilpminder stuck his head out of a window, while Mr Cruet threw open the pilp plant door demanding to know what the hell was going on. From behind the school came a fairy I seemed to recognise. It was the one who dropped the net just before the sprites got through. He began an animated conversation with Mr Cruet, pointing my way every now and then, which seemed to cause Mr Cruet to scowl considerably.

'... so what you're saying is that *she* let them in on purpose ...' I could just make out Mr Cruet's remark above the noise.

By now the sprites were in full view. The sight of such hideous creatures advancing enmasse, were too much for Mrs Flinge, who had just popped round to see what all the fuss was.

She promptly fainted, dropping the cup she was holding and spilling its contents all over the ground.

'You've got a lot to answer for, young lady,' Mr Cruet screamed.

'But Mr Cruet ...,' I shouted above the deafening noise, ' ...you really need to shut the pilp plant door.'

He didn't seem to hear so I made a move to fly down to do it myself.

'Oh no you don't, Lichen.' Gertie seemed to think I was going to her to try and get the bottle back. 'I'm having this drink!' She smirked spitefully and started to hastily unscrew the bottle. She took the lid off in triumph and put the rim to her mouth – and choked fiercely! The greeny-yellow putrid smelling wisp that had been contained in the bottle seized its freedom and floated gently upwards towards its brother.

'Pigging heck, what the hell did you have in there?' Gertie dropped the empty bottle quickly and reached for her nose which she pinched tightly.

'Quickly Gilbert,' called Fred urgently, pointing towards the surging cloak of green that was almost on top of us.

Gilbert spread himself thinly around the outside of the pilp plant, giving himself the best position for attack. Fred took to the roof of the pilpminders where he could shout instructions if need be. I took a front seat on the lower school chimney.

The combination of green, ugly, squeals and the newly arrived smell was too much for the fairy onlookers and they retreated behind the safety of closed doors.

It started the moment I'd sat down. First a few sprites circled round the pilp plant, screeching loudly. The sound of breaking glass could be heard as the windows began to cave in but Gilbert stood firm.

Then one of them yelled, 'dpnf po, nbhjd evtu jo ifsf.' These were obviously the trigger words because a huge array of sprites now descended onto the pilp plant and began to scramble through the broken panes of glass.

Still Gilbert stood firm.

'Gilbert, what are you doing?' screamed Fred. 'You're supposed to be stopping them.' He held his head in his hands in despair.

Still Gilbert stood firm.

It took just a few minutes for all the sprites to clamber through the windows but when the very last one was in, Gilbert drifted upwards. The smell that had encircled the plant now wafted up and into every available crack, gap or hole. Its only visible sign being the greeny-yellow tail it left behind before disappearing inside altogether. Suddenly there was no sound, the screeching had stopped.

From inside, a muttering of voices began.

'xibu uibu tujol?'

The muttering turned to shouting.

'JU EJTHVTUJOH!!'

The shouting turned to shrieking.

'BBBSSSSHHHIIII.' This was panic in any language!

Suddenly there was a mighty crash as the last of the large front windows fell to the ground and shattered. This was followed by a terrified swarm of spluttering, snivelling sprites now desperately fleeing the pilp plant – empty handed. Cursing and whimpering, they flew back towards the crossing exit through which they came. A greeny-yellow wisp followed closely behind as the last one made a frantic scramble to escape its smelly clutches.

'Go on, Gilbert, round them up,' I shouted.

Gilbert gave it one last shot for good measure and flew through the sprite swarm making them fly quicker than they'd ever done before in their lives.

'I'll fly on ahead to open the crossing, Aggie,' called Fred as he dropped from the roof.

I joined the other fairies as we followed behind watching the smell – Gilbert – herd them towards the portal.

As they approached, Gilbert swung upwards and drifted behind some trees. Fred, wearing the biggest pair of sunblockers ever, waited patiently until the last moment then hit the emergency portal button. He leapt from the sun's view. The green mass swarmed through quickly, cursing with every last breath as they passed through.

A stunned silence filled the air as the relief of what had happened hit home.

Phew! The sprites had gone, the magic dust was safe and ...Gertie Cruet was a hero?

Chapter Thirteen

'Well done, Gertie. What a brilliant plan, setting that smelly genie on them,' said Mr Wriddle, patting her on the back. 'You must be so proud,' he added, turning to Mr Cruet who grinned broadly.

'Yes, how did you know that would do it, huh? Genius, pure genius,' said another fairy.

'Well, I-I-I ...' gushed Gertie, pretending to stumble on her words and taking full credit for all that had happened.

Petunia and Violet fluttered excitedly nearby, trying to look over the wings of the growing crowd of fairies who were now congratulating Gertie.

'What's all that about?' asked Gilbert, flying out from behind the trees. He gave his wings a hard shake and smoothed his hair down with his hand. The crown tuft remained aloft.

'Ah, you're back to your old self,' said Fred, removing his sunblockers. 'Although that smell seems to have lingered on you a bit. Phwoa! You need a bath, mate.'

'Why are they all crowding around Gertie?' he whinged. 'Why isn't anyfairy saying "Well done, Gilbert?" to me, Fred?' It hadn't taken Gilbert long, three minutes actually, to slip back into his old moaning ways but this time I could understand.

'Oi,' he shouted to the crowd. 'It was me. I got rid of the sprites not her.'

But they took no notice of him. And Gertie, well she was lapping it up, all giggly and flicking her coarse curly hair from her face.

Fred tried to console him but Gilbert just didn't want to listen.

'I wish I was still a smell, I'd show her. She's a rotten old hag. I hate her!' His voice tailed off as he started wailing. 'You wait Gertie Cruet. I'll get you for this.'

Fred dragged Gilbert off, kicking and screaming, in the direction of home. I began to follow muttering in disbelief. Gertie Cruet a hero indeed!

'And where do you think you're going? I want to talk to you about how you let in the sprites tonight.' The harsh tones of Mr Cruet flew through the air stopping me sharply in my tracks. I turned angrily.

Gasps of disbelief went up from the crowd.

'Aggie Lichen? Well, I never,' came a call.

The whispers among the crowd grew louder and my name kept cropping up closely connected with words like; malicious, spiteful and wicked.

'Let's take her to the school hall and question her,' shouted somefairy.

'Yeah, she needs to pay for all the damage she's caused,' Gertie added, her upper lip curled sneeringly.

The crowd gathered around me, pushing and shoving, arms grabbing at my wings.

'But I didn't let them in on purpose they ...'

'Yeah, yeah, whatever ...' snorted Violet and Petunia together.

Then out of nowhere a familiar voice made everything feel alright – Ma.

'It's okay Aggie, let's get you home,' she said, 'All that trying to save us from those horrid sprites must have clear worn you out,' she added loudly. She grabbed my hand and gave the gobsmacked crowd a last glaring look before flying off.

'But somefairy has to pay for all the damage ...' shouted one brave fairy when Ma was almost out of sight. But she'd heard! She screeched to a halt and flapstopped, plunging us both down directly in front of the fairy who had dared to speak. Ma's precision was perfect.

She stared the fairy straight in the eye, causing him to develop a slight nervous twitch in his left cheek.

'If anyfairy is to pay, perhaps we should be looking to those *brave* fairies who let go of the net in front of the exit!'

The fairy she was staring at gulped loudly and a few others nearby began to cough nervously.

Then we were off again, up and away home where we talked for a while before I could finally get my exhausted head down and go to sleep.

'What a brave little fairy you are, Aggie Lichen,' said Ma, turning off the bedroom light.

'Not so much of the little,' I mumbled sleepily.

****

During the next week most of the talk in the school playground consisted of Gertie Cruet's heroic act and how she had single-handedly saved Pilpsville from the treacherous sprite invasion. And as the week dragged on the tales became more and more embroidered and exaggerated.

'Did you really fight off ten sprites all in one go?' an adoring fan asked.

'Oh yeah,' beamed Gertie, 'and I could only use one arm as the other was injured rescuing a fairylet which had been tied to a dragonfly ...'

I, of course, was given a wide berth because the rest of the gossip centred around how I had apparently let the sprites in on purpose. It was pointless trying to explain so I didn't. The gossip would soon die down when something more interesting came along – like identity of the light!

****

I'd been waiting all week for an opportunity to get into Fred's house to seize the negatives and one had now arisen. Fred's mum wanted to take him to Mrs

Flinge's dress shop on Friday after school to find something 'smart' to wear for the pilpblast.

'I'm only going if you don't go picking out some hideous frilly shirt again,' said Fred.

'But you looked so sweet in it,' said his mum. '... and that little tie ...'

'Mum! You promised!' said Fred.

'And don't you worry, Gilbert. We'll pick something extra special up for you dear.'

Mrs Trickle patted Gilbert's head with one hand whilst holding a kerchief over her mouth with the other.

Gilbert was to stay at home as his mum was still terribly embarrassed about the dreadful smell that still lingered about his person. No amount of rose baths seemed to have worked – he still smelled and he smelled bad! So I was to keep an eye on him.

'Oh, Gilbert, don't forget to put those boxes in the shed.' Mrs Trickle called as she and Fred took off. 'We won't be long, Aggie.'

'No worries, see you later.' Much later I hoped.

I gave them five minutes or so then set about finding the picture negatives. I'd sent Gilbert out in the garden to play with the dragonflies. It also gave me some relief from the terrible smell that trailed after him.

Fred's bedroom was the most likely place so I started there. His room was not unlike Albert's; messy and smelly, although not as dirty. The blue paint on the walls was peeling in places, the decaying enamel showing underneath. A large tree carved bed sat in front of the window. Beech tree shelves lined two of the walls and were crammed full of old papers and books on aerodynamics. I carefully flicked through them just in case, before going through Fred's school bag that lay on the floor. I searched the obvious places like the drawers, in the wardrobe and under the bed. Phew, what was that smell?

'What'ya doing?' Blast and damnation! Gilbert stood in the doorway, arms folded, leaning against the doorframe.

'Err, just looking for something I left behind last week,' I muttered feebly.

'What was that then?'

'Err, some picture negatives. Do you know where they might be?' Well I'd been caught red-handed so what the hell!

'Oh those, yeah, try under the mattress. Fred always keeps his secret stuff there.' He gave me a shrewd smile then disappeared back into the garden.

'Don't forget to put those boxes in the shed,' I called after him.

Sure enough, there under the mattress amongst various other bits and bobs were the negatives. Great! I held them up to the light, trying to see if they revealed anything suspicious but as I did so, an awful stench filled the air once more.

'Oh, you found them then.' Gilbert was back again!

'Did you want something, Gilbert?' Like a bath!

'It's just ... well, there's a really strange noise coming from the shed.'

I shoved the negatives quickly into my pocket and let go of the mattress.

'...a *really, really,* strange noise ...'

It was then that the scrap of paper caught my eye.

'...yes, okay and it's coming from the shed, I know. I'll be there in a minute.' When I'd had a quick look at the piece of paper. It looked as if had been scrunched up into a ball then smoothed out again. What could have been so important about it that Fred felt the need to keep it with his special stuff? Picking it up, I could hardly believe my eyes. The paper was filled with doodles and sketches which were all in a similar vein ...

A tapping noise came from outside. Great! They must have come back. The tapping became banging, accompanied by a frantic whispering. 'Aggie, Aggie!'

It was Gilbert but I couldn't see him anywhere.

'Gilbert, stop messing about. Where are you?'

'I'm outside the window. Open the curtains, quick.' His voice was edged with anxiety.

I threw open the curtains. 'This had better be good, Gilbert.'

He was balancing on a rickety old wooden box. His hands clung tightly to the window ledge. He looked terribly worried, 'You really had better come – now.'

Chapter Fourteen

'What?' I demanded to know.

Gilbert jumped down from the box and ran over to the shed. 'In there. I was trying to find a place to stack the boxes ...'

'Well that was a good idea, well done. You've put them in the shed. Now can we go back in? I want to get to the library as soon as your mum's back.' As I turned to go back inside, he pulled my arm fiercely.

'I was going to put them in the blue wardrobe, you know the one ...'

'Yeah, yeah, yeah, get on with it.' We were nearing the shed door as he finished his sentence.

'...anyway, when I opened the wardrobe door I found it in the corner.'

'You found what in the corner?'

He opened the shed door hesitantly and shuffled uneasily towards the wardrobe.

'This!' He used a broom to prise open the door and pointed warily to a dark corner.

'Okay, so what exactly am I looking at here? Is it a spider? If you've bought me out here for a spider ...'

A strange non-spider murmuring came from within. Two large eyes appeared from the darkness immediately followed by two huge ears and an enormous mouth.

'bssshhhiii,' it screamed.

'Arrrgggghhh,' I screamed.

The wardrobe door slammed noisily as I leapt out of the shed. A muffled shrieking noise, coming from the wardrobe, could just be heard.

'Ssshh! I think you've frightened it,' said Gilbert.

'You're having a laugh aren't you? There's a flipping sprite in the wardrobe and you're worried I might have upset it? Well, that takes the cracker.'

'I think it got left behind when they invaded.'

'Oh, you don't say! – Look, there's a sprite in your shed and you'd better shift it quick.'

'How? What am I going to do with it? Besides it's an orphan so it's got no one to look after it.' He kicked a stone carelessly against the shed.

'Well, that's tough! Find somewhere ... what d'ya mean it's an orphan? How'd you know?'

'It told me,' he said sheepishly.

'You've been chatting with it ... in spritespiel?'

'Well, yeah. I can sort of understand him. I think it's something to do with having been a smell, some sort of greeny sameness. Oh, and he's called wjdups.'

'HE's called what? whdvps? What kind of a name is that?' I asked sarcastically.

'It's wjdups! Roughly translated – it's – err – it's Victor!'

'Victor, huh! Well, tell Victor the sprite to be on his way before I get my catapult out again.'

The shrieks in the wardrobe grew louder.

'It's all right Victor, the nasty fairy doesn't mean it. Seriously Aggie, what shall we do?'

'Well, I promised your mum I'd stay here and I certainly can't leave whjpds...'

'wjdups!' interrupted Gilbert.

'Can I? So you'll have to go ... and find Bessie.'

'Shall I get Myrtle too? I expect she'll want to come too.'

'No! Just get Bessie and be quick or I might just be tempted to ...'

'Okay, I'm gone.' And he most certainly was.

I couldn't risk the neighbours finding *Victor*, they'd hang him out to dry, so I pulled the door tightly closed and locked it. I gave it a quick tug just to be sure.

I ran back inside the house and rushed to the front door, flinging it wide open. Good, no sign of Fred or his mum. Phew! One less thing to think about.

I made sure Fred's room was in the same state, messy and dirty, before returning to the shed at the bottom of the garden.

There was a faint whimpering as I opened the door.

'SSSHHH, spritey, somefairy might hear. What's the matter, are you hungry?' I cooed.

The creature in the wardrobe hissed and spat viciously as I approached.

'Ah, look. Aggie's talking to the poor little thing.' Gilbert stood in the shed doorway, smirking.

'Stupid sprite! I was just trying to be friendly but IT won't have it.'

'Is he all right? You haven't done anything to him, have you?' said Gilbert, frowning at me like a teacher who hadn't received their homework on time.

'Oh shut up, Gilbert and do tell me why Bugface is here. I said get Bessie, not get Bugface. She'll tell everyone … and why've you got my laundry basket?'

'Bessie said we should bring it and I couldn't really ask your mum for a cage to put a SPRITE in, now could I?' he whispered through gritted teeth. 'Don't worry, Myrtle emptied all your smelly socks out first.' With that he pushed past me dragging the laundry basket behind him and made for the wardrobe.

I joined Bessie and Bugface outside. We leant against the shed while we waited for Gilbert to do his thing.

'You are sure it's a sprite, aren't you, Aggie?' said Bessie.

'Well, yeah. It's green and small and speaks in spritespiel. What else could it be?' I said, picking a shed splinter out of my hand.

'You're sure it's a greeny colour and not a yucky browny colour, aren't you?' She gave a shudder as she spoke.

'Bess, I do know the difference between a sprite and a Grublin!'

CRASH!

'What was that?' said Bugface.

A shrill cry came from inside the shed. It was followed by sounds of a fierce struggle between a tooth fairy and a sprite that was obviously trying to resist being shoved into a laundry basket.

'Right, that's it Gilbert. I'm coming in,' I shouted.

I moved to the back of the shed and could see Gilbert on all fours, scrambling around on the floor. Victor had escaped.

'wjdups, wjdups, here wjdups.'

'Crikey, Gilbert, you'll be telling it to 'stay' soon.'

'I'm just trying to call him – Victor, come on, Victor.' There was a scratching sound from behind the grasscutter, followed by 'ppqt!' A small green head emerged slowly with a rather embarrassed look on its small green face.

'j ibe b mjuumf bddjefou,' it blubbed.

I looked at Gilbert who was reaching behind the grasscutter and successfully retrieving a *very* small and somewhat damp sprite by its ear. Its face appeared somewhat ridiculous as the size of its eyes and mouth had completely taken over. There was little space left for anything like cheeks, chin or forehead. It was a masterpiece of confusion.

'What's he say?' I said, grabbing the laundry basket as I got nearer.

'He seems to have had a 'little accident'. He's terribly embarrassed about it.' Gilbert reached out for the basket, said something in spritespiel to Victor and dropped him in the basket, shutting the lid quickly. Gilbert breathed a sigh of relief, which was to be short lived as his mother stormed into the shed.

'Ah, so this is where you're both hiding. Which one of you left the front door open? There's a swarm of gnats in the kitchen, all over the petal pudding.'

'I'm so sorry, Mrs Trickle. It was ... Gilbert. He was trying to get some fresh air into the house, you know – because of the smell. Isn't that right, Gilbert dear?' I pulled him roughly in front of me and held him by the shoulders.

'Yes, that's right, Aggie.' Gilbert smiled at his mother through clenched teeth. 'Just trying to clear the air a little.' He stepped back, crushing all life out of my left foot.

'Right, well ... both of you, in the kitchen – and you Fred ... and get rid of those gnats.'

She stomped back up the path, cursing under her breath. Fred traipsed after her, taking Bessie and Myrtle with him.

'I think we got away with it, Aggie dear,' said Gilbert sarcastically, pulling away from me.

'Don't you 'Aggie dear' me, you little devil.' He ducked quickly as I took a swipe at his left earlobe.

'Well, you should have told the truth, after all, you left the door open,' he said.

'Aren't you forgetting the rest? Like how you've got a sprite hidden in your mum's shed, Gilbert dear!'

He turned, poked out his tongue and ran swiftly up the garden path.

'Why you little ...'

A loud squealing came from the far corner of the shed where the laundry basket was. It rocked and swayed to the point of teetering over as its contents pushed and shoved from the inside.

'Oh, no you don't, spritey.' I pushed it back into the blue wardrobe then placed a couple of the large boxes on top. 'That should do it.'

'Come on Aggie, help us out,' Fred shouted from the back door.

'All right, I'm coming!' The key turned in the lock and a quick tug confirmed that the door was shut. I headed back up the garden path.

'Quick, throw me that can of Gnat Splat®,' called Mrs Trickle.

I grabbed the blackened can from behind the rickety crate that Gilbert had stood on when he first discovered Victor.

'Not much in it,' I said, shaking the can vigorously.

'The can, please!'

'Sorry, Mrs Trickle.' I passed over the can of Gnat Splat® which she quickly sprayed inside the house. 'Right, that should do it.' She threw the empty can in the bin. 'Next time, keep the door shut.'

Gilbert and I looked at the ground sheepishly as she vanished inside the now gnat free zone. Shortly afterwards, Fred's head appeared at the bedroom window. 'So what the hell was all that about?' he mouthed. He gestured at me to come in.

'Not you, Gilbert. Go and find Myrtle.'

Bessie was already in the room. She started filling Fred in on what had happened. His face contorted as the word 'sprite' was mentioned.

'So, it's in my shed? My shed!'

'It's just a temporary measure,' I said, 'You know, 'til we find somewhere else.'

'Well, how the hell did it get there in the first place?'

'Sshh, your mum'll hear,' Bessie shoved him as she spoke. 'Who knows how it got here? It just did.'

'So what are we going to do with him?' I said.

'Hmm, Hmm,' Gilbert's face appeared at the door.

'I told you to find Myrtle …'

'I did and she said it's okay if he goes to yours for a while, just until we decide what to do with him,' said Gilbert.

Bugface appeared at the doorway and looked at the ground, shuffling her feet uneasily.

'Well, you'll have to take responsibility for him. I've got enough to worry about without that as well.'

'So it's all right then?' Bugface looked at me cautiously.

'Like I said, Bugface, it's down to you. I really have got to get going now.'

'Where are you going in such a hurry? Do you want me to come?' asked Bessie.

'No, you take Bugface home to find a place for Victor.'

I had some important research to do ... in the library.

Chapter Fifteen

Thanks to the problems with Victor and the gnats, I'd only left myself an hour before the library shut. Miss Jowl, the keeper of books, was seated at the huge wooden desk that confronted each borrower as they entered through the large – now cracked – glass doors. She was flicking diligently through a wad of tickets, her glasses – also cracked – poised on the end of her thin, pointed nose. On hearing footsteps she looked up from her duties, pushing her glasses back into the correct position.

'Hello Agnes, I haven't seen you for a while. How have you been?' she asked politely.

Now, did I tell her how I'd really been – flapstopping, losing the dress, Gilbert the smell, letting the sprites in, finding out who the light really was …

'I've been fine,' I replied politely.

'I am glad to hear it. Now what can I do for you?'

'I just wanted to use one of the enlargers, if that's okay.'

'Well, under normal circumstances it certainly would be okay…'

'What do you mean 'normal circumstances'? I thought they were for everyfairy to use …' I interrupted.

'Under normal circumstances they *would* be available to anyfairy who wanted to use them. Unfortunately the sprite invasion has rendered them useless.' She pointed to a far corner of the library where pieces of broken glass had been swept into a neat pile.

Damn, no enlargers!

'Is there nothing else I could use, Miss Jowl?'

'I'm sorry Agnes, I have ordered new ones but there is a six week delivery period.'

'Oh, okay.' That was about as much use as a pilp sack with a hole in it! I turned to leave, bitterly disappointed.

'Hold on Agnes, I may be able to help after all. There is an old one somewhere in the basement if I remember rightly.' She tapped her head with her fingers. 'Yes, I am sure I kept one back. It's made of plastic so shouldn't have been damaged. I'll just pop down and have a look.' She disappeared through a nearby door eager to please, as always.

It was a good ten minutes before she emerged. Her hair, which was piled in a bun, was slightly out of place and covered in dust and cobwebs. Her glasses hung around her neck on a piece of coloured string and she was most definitely grasping something in her hand.

'It's a little dusty but from what I can see it does work,' she said, coughing and wiping her hands on an old piece of cloth. 'I hope it's of some use, Agnes.'

'Thanks Miss Jowl, I really appreciate it. Can I take it through to the study section?'

She looked down her glasses at me, 'Are you sure you know where that is?'

Well, it had been a while since I'd used it. 'I'm sure I'll remember the way,' I said.

Wow! At last, an enlarger. This would either confirm or disprove my suspicions.

The study area was empty. Friday wasn't exactly a popular day for studying in Pilpsville. As I set the enlarger up, I was filled with an uneasy feeling as my stomach turned over and over. In a few short moments the identity of the light would be revealed at last.

I rummaged around in my bag for the negatives and pictures, all there bar two – which Fettock had. I started to examine them closely, my heart pounding with a mixture of excitement and anxiety.

My hands were shaking as I placed the first negative under the enlarger. It wasn't of much use – very blurry and revealed no more than it had before. My relief was short lived, however, as the next one and the one after that and indeed every other picture exposed *it* in all it's glory. The tubes, two strapped together, were just as I'd seen in the detailed plan in his bedroom. This was the proof I'd been dreading I'd find. There was no doubt in my mind now. It was my brother. It was Albert! He was *the light*.

****

Quite how I arrived home I'm not sure. Perhaps I was on auto-pilot. It was like some terrible nightmare. How was I going to break the news to Ma and Pa? And what about Myrtle, how would she take it? Gertie Cruet would be in her element when she found out.

Albert – I still couldn't believe it. How could he do such a thing? When I thought about all the nightsgritches he was 'too busy' to go on! Oh he'd been there all right but in a different form. And making all those poor fairies drop their pilp sacks. But worst of all causing his own sister to flapstop like that – no wonder he'd arrived so quickly to take Myrtle home! Oh hell, what was I to do?

'Aggie, dinner's ready,' called Pa.

He was sat at the table opposite me, a rare occasion of him actually being in. I stared as nastily as I could. He just smirked. Well he would I suppose, not knowing that I knew all about his mean and disgraceful tricks.

'Eat your dinner properly please Aggie. That is if you can fit it in between scowling!' Ma frowned as she refilled her plate with beash and carrbot stew.

But the scowl on my face remained and became a permanent fixture as I ate silently through the rest of the meal. He finished before me and left the table.

'What's Albert up to tonight, Ma?' I asked innocently.

'He's off on the nightsgritch, Aggie. You know that.'

I had to be sure. Well, I'd be watching him real close from now on – as close as I could get without being caught.

I found Myrtle in the bedroom sorting out her clothes ready for the evening ahead. I wrestled with my secret, wanting to share my thoughts with someone – even Myrtle.

She kept nipping in and out of the room, each time coming back with her pockets bulging with bits of food and then unloading them into a plastic container. I had to ask!

'What the heck are you doing? We've only just eaten. Surely you can't still be hungry?'

'It's for Victor, you know.' She nodded towards the cupboard. 'He must be starved.'

'Tell me you're kidding? I mean, you put him in the cupboard? He's in the basket still isn't he?'

'Well, yeah! I'm not stupid you know.'

'And the lid's still on, yeah? Only there's something under the bed and it's trying to have my leg for dinner!'

'I told you he was hungry. Come on, Victor, I've

got some food for you.' She dangled some bits of carrbot below the bed.

A green hand made a grab for them and there followed a disgusting gobbling sound as the sprite gulped down the scraps of vegetables. A small green head popped out and carefully looked around.

'tpnf npsf, qmfbtf.' He gestured towards his mouth.

'Oh look, Aggie, he wants some more. He's so cute.'

Great! I had a cheat for a brother, an idiot for a sister and a sprite for a pet.

Could things get any worse?

'By the way, Fred wants to see you urgently,' Bugface added casually.

Err, yes – they certainly could!

'I'll probably see him tonight anyway. I'm sure there's no real rush. We're supposed to be going to the juice bar with Bessie. That's of course if I've got any credits left.' I fumbled around in my pockets, not much there just the negatives and THE PIECE OF PAPER!!! As I unfolded the scrap I'd hastily shoved in my pocket I realised exactly why Fred wanted to see me urgently – the rough sketch of the two tube thingy. Fred had also discovered Albert's secret.

'What about the nightsgritch, shouldn't we be collecting really tonight?' I needed a good excuse to get out of meeting Fred.

'No, it's our night off, remember? Albert's working

tonight – if he ever gets out of his bedroom.'

He's probably making some final adjustments to his two tube thingy, I thought, before he encounters his next poor victim and relieves them of their well earned pilps.

'Bessie's here, Aggie,' Ma interrupted, calling from the kitchen. 'I'm sending her through.'

'Better get Victor away, Bugface, just in case Ma comes in.'

She carefully placed Victor back into the laundry basket, complete with a handful of vegetable scraps but it didn't stop him from taking a chunk out of my finger.

'Ouch, why me? I helped to save you.'

There was a soft knock on the door just as Myrtle replaced the lid.

'It's only me.' It was Bessie.

'And me,' – with Gilbert!

'Quick, we were just giving Victor some food although he seems to prefer eating me for some reason.' I held out my finger for all to see.

Gilbert lifted the lid and started talking to Victor in spritespiel. I tried desperately to think up an excuse for not meeting up with Fred but Bessie insisted.

'Come on, Aggie. We haven't been out properly for ages and Mrs Cheric has concocted some really exciting juices up especially for tonight.'

'But I'm exhausted, Bessie, what with Victor and

that.' – and Albert being a cheat and a thief.

'And Fred needs to see you urgently …' There it was again – Fred needed to see me urgently,

'… about the selling of the pilp plant …' The pilp plant sale – blow, I'd forgotten about that.

'… and apparently there's only ten days left to put a stop to it,' Bessie continued.

So that's what he wanted – but why did he have the drawing?

'Ready then?'

'Can I meet you there in five minutes? I just need to change my clothes.'

'Okay,' said Bessie – and Myrtle – and Gilbert – with a rather large lump under his jumper,

'plbz,' – and Victor!

As soon as they had left the room I hid the incriminating piece of paper out of sight in the cupboard and quickly changed into my going out clothes. There was no sign of Albert as I left the house, which was probably a good thing.

****

I arrived at the juice bar just a few minutes after the gang. It was really busy tonight. I spotted Bessie and the others at our usual table by the window where we would watch the world go by. There were other small groups of fairies sitting around chatting and enjoying the strange juices Mrs Cheric had been concocting.

I acknowledged a heavily scarf clad Phyllis sitting in the far corner with another fairy. I couldn't see who it was as he or she had their back to me but they were having a really heated discussion about something or other. There was a lot of shaking of heads and glaring going on with a few fist thumps thrown in for good measure. Ah well, none of my business.

'Sorry I took so long, guys. Have I missed much?' I asked getting myself comfy on a stool. I looked across the table and glanced at Fred who greeted me with a quick smile.

'We were just saying that what with there only being ten days left we really have got to make more of an effort to stop Arty Granger,' said Bessie sounding very serious indeed!

'And Fred thinks he knows something,' said Gilbert, in between mouthfuls of rose and spinach surprise. The bulge under his clothing was moving around a lot and he was having problems controlling it. Every now and then Gilbert stuffed a daisy cookie up his jumper much to the amusement of other juice drinkers nearby.

'Be careful, you'll get caught and then there'll be trouble. Let me have him for a while,' I whispered, putting my hand out to try and get hold of the sprite.

But this was met with much squealing from within the jumper.

'Okay, okay. Just quieten him down will you? Fairies are looking!' Quite what I'd done to offend him I didn't know but he'd obviously taken a dislike to me.

'The thing is Aggie, I think I've discovered something about the light,' Fred whispered, his head hanging low.

'O-Oh right, I-I see. Perhaps we could talk about this outside.'

'… and I have a hunch that it's something to do with the selling of the pilp plant.'

'… outside would be really good for me. I'm feeling rather hot and bothered.' I started to get up and moved towards the door, absentmindedly bumping into another fairy in my hurry.

'Oops, sorry. I just needed some fresh …' I stopped in my tracks, mouth dropping open as Arty Granger angrily pushed past me.

Oh heck I wonder if he'd overheard us. No, he was the type to speak his mind but that seemed preoccupied at the moment!

'Aggie, for crying out loud, can you just sit still for a minute. Let me just explain what I mean unless of course you've got a better reason for it all.'

I had but I was sure as hell not sharing it with anyone here!

'Okay! I'm listening.' … and when I don't like what I hear I'm going!

'I have reason to believe that somefairy we know

is the light and is helping Arty Granger.'

'Look, you've got no proof.' And, he hadn't. I'd made sure of that. 'Besides you can't just go around accusing fairies like that.'

'I know that. I'm just saying how else could he have got the credits to buy the plant. It makes sense, surely.' He looked at me, waiting for an answer of some kind.

'What are you lot looking at? I'm not the light, am I?'

'op, tif't uif cbe gbjsz,' came a muffled comment from Gilbert's jumper.

'Sssshhh, Victor.' Gilbert tapped his stomach. Mrs Cheric threw a strange look across the room to him.

'No pets in here, Gilbert Trickle, you know that,' she called from behind the counter, fighting off a lissell plant that had become attached to her hair.

'It's just my stomach rumbling,' he retorted. She threw him another look for good measure.

'No, that's not what I'm saying,' said Fred, flaying his arms around so much that Myrtle's pish blossom squash wobbled dangerously at the edge of the table.

'Think about all the pilps that have been lost – or stolen – on account of the light,' he added.

'Look, Albert has already explained what the light really is, hasn't he? Even Fettock knows that, doesn't he?'

'Perhaps that story was enough to keep some fairies quiet but let's face it, it doesn't take a genius to know what's really going on.' He looked around at the blank faces that looked back at him, including a small green one that had popped out of Gilbert's jumper and was promptly pushed back in again.

'Okay, maybe I haven't explained as fully as I should have. What I'm saying is this – every time the light appears, pilp sacks full of pilps get dropped. I think that the light is giving those sacks full of pilps to Arty Granger so that he can buy the pilp plant.'

'But what would he – it – have to gain from that?' This was so much worse than I had first thought. Why would Albert want to help Arty Granger like that? He knew what it would mean to the community. He must be getting a percentage of the profits – how else could he have afforded the parts to make the two tube thingy.

'Look I'm not saying I've got all the answers but unless any of you have got anything else to share…'

'SSSSSllluuurrpp!' Gilbert drained the last dregs of his second drink, a girgberry surprise, noisily, totally disinterested in what Fred was saying.

'…I think this is the way to go …'

'Oooops, pardon me!' Still disinterested, Gilbert belched loudly.

'boe nf!' A second belch came from the jumper.

'...if we're going to solve the problem ...' Fred waited for a moment, glared at Gilbert expectantly then continued, '...and put a stop to Arty's game.'

'What about your 'friend'? Has he come up with anything?' asked Bessie.

'What 'friend'? I thought it was just us involved,' I said.

'I just asked somefairy to look into a couple of things for me, you know,' said Fred.

Friend? I know just who his 'friend' was – Fettock! How on earth was I to get Albert out of this mess now?

The evening wore on and I fought hard to stay calm and stop Albert's name slipping off my tongue. I was actually pleased when Mrs Cheric announced last orders so that I could escape my friends and return to the safety of my bedroom.

'Aren't you forgetting something?' Fred called out as I tried to make my get away.

Gilbert lifted his jumper up.

Victor looked at me and whined, 'j epo'u xbou up hp xjui uif cbe gbjsz ...'

'He keeps saying that,' said Gilbert.

'Keeps saying what?' asked Myrtle, taking the sprite from him.

'Something about Aggie being the bad fairy.'

'Oh, cheers. We take him in and I'm the bad fairy. Come On, Bugface – and bring cabbage face with you.'

I made some excuses about needing to get back home quickly, leaving the others carry on 'the investigation' by themselves.

'Let's meet up in a couple of days, Aggie. I should have an answer to it all by then,' Fred called as we left.

No fear! School seasonal break would give me the perfect opportunity to avoid Fred while I carried out my own investigation – stalking Albert. I had to know, I had to see for myself. Then I would reveal the truth, the awful truth, to the family.

Chapter Sixteen

The following morning started early with a mixture of muffled wailing, whinging and tapping on the cupboard door. Victor wanted out.

'Oi, Myrtle, wake up. Cabbage breath's awake.' I gave her a shove. 'Myrtle!'

She let out a loud throaty snore and turned over.

'Great! I suppose I'll have to deal with him.'

He'd already thrown the lid off and as I opened the door he was standing up in the laundry basket all green and pathetic looking.

'What? What do you want?' I said.

'opu zpv!' With that he poked out his long green tongue, jumped straight out of the basket and hurtled passed me to get to Myrtle. I made a move to grab him as he jumped on the bed but he scrambled quickly under her pillow. Well, his head did. The rest of him was stuck up in the air for all to see.

'Oh, you little ...'

I was distracted by a noise from the kitchen. I took a quick peek – Albert.

Hmm, he was up early! Time for me to get dressed and put my plan into action. I would follow his every move.

Myrtle sat up sleepily, trying to bash the large lump out of her pillow.

'Why're you up and dressed so early?' she yawned.

'Ask the cabbage under your pillow!'

Closing the bedroom door quietly I followed Albert as he made for the front door. I watched from behind the trees as he flew down the street towards the centre of town. He passed Bessie's where he greeted her mum with a polite 'Good Morning'. I followed closely. Then down past the pilp plant where an orderly queue had formed outside the main door. Friday was a busy day for pilp exchanging, especially with the pilpblast coming up next week. He headed towards the general store. Perhaps he had a secret meeting with Arty there, or perhaps he was just – buying a paper for Pa? What was he doing, acting all normal like?

'Good morning, Aggie,' Mr Wriddle called to the tree I was supposedly hiding behind.

'M-M-Morning,' I mumbled, retreating once more. Blimey, I was rubbish at spying.

'Morning, Aggie,' said Albert. Damn, that confirmed it. 'What are you up to? Do you want to get a juice at Mrs Cheric's?'

'Err, no! Haven't you got other things to do, like?'

'No, I was just getting Pa's paper for him. You sure about that juice?'

'Yeah, I've got to get to the, to the, err, library so I can't stop. Bye!'

I waited until he'd turned the corner and started to follow him once more. This went on for several boring hours with me jumping from tree to tree in an effort to avoid being spotted. He spent a lot of time in the juice bar drinking what looked like blickberry and prea slush. Then he popped into bakers and emerged with a bag of crose cakes. The highlight of the day was his visit to the wing servicer, where he spent twenty minutes, according to my notebook. It was hopeless. I decided that my time might be better spent asking around for any news from last nightsgritch but nofairy remembered seeing the light.

Perhaps he knew I was on to him and had kept his head down. It was only later on that day that I began to gather some real evidence. I flew past Phyllis Router's house on my way home and bumped into Phyllis herself.

'Hey, Phyllis. How are you?' I asked, trying not to stare rudely at the scarf which was attempting to hide her bulging eyes, grey skin – and now even longer nose.

'Well I'mm feelingg quite relievedd actually,' she said.

'What do you mean, relievedd, err, relieved?'

'Well, I'mm just soo glad I wasn'tt on thee nightsgritchh last night. I heardd that thatt wretched light wass out againn and twoo Canningford fairies lostt their whole sackss of pilps.'

Oh hell, he'd been at it again after all. I needed to get home quick to try and find the pilps. Two sacks, huh!

'They're bothh in a terrible state off shockk,' she continued.

'Oh, right. Well I'm sorry to hear that but – err, I must dash.' I left Phyllis in mid flow. Blimey, if that's what shock did to you, she really should get herself to a healer!

My thoughts then returned to Albert as I rushed to reach home before he got back. But my search for pilp sacks proved fruitless. What a waste of time!

In fact the next week – supposedly a break from school – was much the same I'd rather have been in school in actual fact. I spent most of my time either stalking Albert or avoiding Fred. It was exhausting!

Albert, well I couldn't believe what a boring life he led. And what with Fred sending dragonfly messages to the house, it was all a bit much. By Friday though, I could no longer avoid him. He arrived at my house just after lunch, together with Gilbert to check on Victor's well being. Gilbert shot off to find Myrtle leaving me and Fred alone – awkwardly!

'Have you been avoiding me, Aggie?' he asked.

'I-I-I've just been really busy helping with the pilpblast and that. In fact I've got to shoot off now. I'll catch up with you later, Fred,' I said, grabbing my jacket off the wall hook.

'Not so quick, Aggie ...'

We were interrupted by Gilbert. 'Where's Myrtle? Where's Victor? I can't find them,' he whinged.

'Try the garden,' I muttered. Gilbert slammed the door as his brother Fred continued his verbal assault on me.

'But time's running out, Aggie. The thirtieth day is tomorrow, you know, the day of the pilpblast. Great timing, huh?'

'Well, I'm tied up with something else at the moment. Just give me a little more ...'

The door bounced open and crashed noisily into the kitchen wall.

'They're not in the garden. I can't find them and I want to see Victor.' Gilbert had returned and had a face on him like a bag of squirrel nuts.

'Go and look in the tree dwelling, in fact just GO!' I screamed.

'Ooooo, touchy,' he said, running off quickly.

'I know, Aggie,' Fred continued, 'I've known for a while now.'

'I'm sorry ... but you know what?' I looked at him disguising my fear with a feigned blank expression.

'I know who the light is and its involvement with the pilp plant sale.' He smoothed back his hair as he spoke. The irritating crown tuft remained aloft.

'Oh shut up, Fred. You always think you know all the answers, don't you? Why don't you just mind your own business this time,' I said crossly.

'It is my business, Aggie,' he scowled angrily. 'It's everyone's business. You've got to listen to me if we're going to put a stop to it all.'

'Just push off, Fred, like I said, I've got things to do.' As I turned to leave he grabbed my arm tightly. I needed to go. Albert had just taken off and I had to follow quickly.

'Look, I know this is hard for you, Aggie but it's got to be done. I've sent a friend off to track Arty's movements. We should catch them both together tonight making the final deal then we'll have our evidence. Meet me at the juice bar at 8'0'clock. We'll go together.'

We both looked down at my arm which was now turning a bright shade of red where his grip was so tight.

'S-S-Sorry, I …'

'Crikey, are you hard of hearing?' I pulled my arm away. 'I said I'm busy.' I hurled my final remark at him and flew off out the door, flying swiftly in an effort to catch up with Albert. I'd overheard him telling Ma that he had something important to do and so couldn't help with the final pilpblast preparations. I needed to see what he was up to for myself.

Damn Fred, I thought, damn interfering busybody. His words were ringing in my ears as I followed Albert into town again. 'I know who the light is, Aggie, I know who it is.'

No, I would *not* be meeting him tonight. My intention was to confront Albert before any other fairy caught him. We could then sort this whole mess out together, after all there had to be some kind of explanation.

I followed hard on his wings. Albert visited the local shops as before and took time out to go to the juice bar. Sitting in the window, he made notes in a little book he kept in his pocket.

I perched myself on a nearby hoak tree as I waited for him to finish his drink. It was quite a fine spot to fairy watch and made a change from our usual place.

Mr Wriddle flew by clutching a newspaper under his arm. On the bench, Miss Thrune sat reading a book called 'How to Get the Best from Your Pupils'. A few of my classmates also flew by including Phyllis Router, the rotten liar although she could hardly been deemed a classmate – really.

My eyes passed from Phyllis to the juice bar door. Albert emerged. He looked all around him as if to make sure the coast was clear then took off. I dropped down from the tree ready to go and … found myself face to face with Bessie.

'What are you up to, Aggie?' she asked, glaring at me suspiciously.

'I can't say and I can't stop, sorry.' I flew up, urgently needing to find where Albert had disappeared to.

'But Aggie ...,' she called after me but her voice trailed off and became a distant echo as I made my way up higher.

Ahead I could just make out Albert still climbing high and pushing towards the lush surroundings of Great Molaring, just as expected. He moved swiftly and as he entered the town began to duck in and out of the houses and the trees. This made it very difficult to keep up with him.

'Oh, for goodness sake. Now where's he got to?' I muttered under my breath, just a little frustrated to have come so far and ... 'Ah, there he is.' I spotted him leaning against the back door of a large white enamel house with long green shutters, his head pressed tightly to it as if listening for something. A house as big as that – it must have been Arty Granger's house. A sudden noise in the road behind made me turn, and in that split second Albert was gone again.

I swung around the green shuttered house but there was no sign of him. Flipping heck, he certainly wasn't making things easy for me. Then a glint of light caught my eye and, on looking up, I was pleasantly surprised to see him up and flying off once more.

This time I wouldn't allow myself to be distracted – not even by a very unusual dragonfly that had just passed.

'Damn, I've done it again!' I thought, 'Now where … ah.' He was clearly in my sights once more. This time I followed tightly as he left the borders of Great Molaring and headed for … and headed for … Pigging hell – Grublin City!!

Chapter Seventeen

Now Grublin City was not a place you went to voluntarily. More likely you went there if you were kidnapped, stumbled accidentally into it or had to go there for a dare. It was a place best avoided after dark, during the day and well, basically at all times in between. It was a place where even the suns were afraid to go leaving it permanently dark and dingy. It was a place where nofairy should go alone so what the hell was Albert doing? Come to think of it, what the hell was I doing?

The smell was the first thing and, indeed, the only thing that ran out to greet you. It was the most foul, sewage smelling stench that could ever be imagined. And it sneaked slyly into every available orifice. It didn't seem to bother Albert though, who was just ahead but had yet to enter the city. He'd landed near a gnarled old tree just outside the city wall. The stinking mud gurgled excitedly around his ankles. It seemed to be all that was left of the River Grub. He smeared the mud over his clothes and spread it thinly around his wings. I looked for a similar puddle and keeping one eye on Albert, I smeared myself with mud. It squelched through my fingers and I heaved as the smell hit me once again.

It wasn't long before Albert was off again. I followed low, close and smelling awful, as he approached the huge wooden gates where a Grublin stood guard at the city's entrance. In the old days, when there really was a River Grub, the walls were just for show as anything could fly over them. Now, however, you risked instant death from the poisonous smelly river fumes that hung precariously above the city. The only way in, as I was about to find out, was through the city gate.

The guard put his grey grubby hand out as Albert tried to pass. He stood taller than a pilp collector and was probably double the width. His clothes were a hotchpotch of styles and grubby colours that were held together tightly in the middle by a large buckled belt. All this was topped by a typical Grublin face; little bulging eyes, pointed, but very small, ears, a strangely cute mouth and the longest nose I'd ever seen. It reached the creature's chin and had three nostrils! The Grublin stepped closer to Albert and began to sniff the air around him. This was where the mud played its part, disguising the fairy smell. Albert thrust something shiny under the hideous creature's nose. The Grublin seemed to like it and snatched it greedily, depositing it hastily into its coat pocket. He waved Albert on. Now it was my turn. I made a move to leave the safety of the tree I was behind and by a pure stroke of luck a group of Grublins passed by the tree. Without thinking I quickly tagged onto the back. They didn't seem to notice as they were too busy arguing. Each one of them dropped something shiny into the guards hand as they passed through. Hmm, what did I have? Just a sparkly hairgrip but he seemed to accept it gladly. The group moved on and I was just congratulating myself on my prowess when a shout came up from the gate.

'Oii whichh onee off youu Grubss givedd mee diss, huhh??' He was waving a grubby fist in the air and shouting, 'Youu gett backk heree youu littlee swiness.' The Grublins turned and laughed muttering something him being a 'madd oldd twitt before dispersing leaving me, a thirteen year old pilp collector, completely and utterly alone.

Alone in a city I had never been to before, something I wouldn't wish on my worst enemy – oops, that was *so* untrue – and I smelled like hell. But then again, so did the rest of the city. Whirling through every dark alley, of which there were many, was a thick brown putrid fog. The tall gas lamps highlighted each one carefully with its own eerie shadow. The alleys opened onto streets which were just an extension, it would seem, of the River Grub itself – damp, muddy with a continuous trickle of water.

A variety of buildings lined the streets all of which were brick built, presumably with mud from the river which only added to the fragrant aroma! They were designed in no particular way at all. It seemed as if someone had just found an empty spot, threw some bricks in and nailed up a door. Gaping holes in the roofs acted as primitive chimneys and windows were definitely in short supply here. Many buildings leant to one side. Many leant forwards. Many leant on each other! I presumed that these were Grublin homes, based purely on the fact that the buildings with windows had things displayed inside and were therefore – shoppes! Inside these buildings, Grublins fought greedily over the few grubby items the shop contained. Some disputes spilling out noisily onto the streets knocking Grublin passer-bys flying.

I was becoming distracted. I had to think quickly, I had to focus. Questions formed in my head; what was I doing here? What did I need to look for?

Albert – he was meeting Arty and I needed to find something to do with metal, like on the two tube thingy. I looked for Albert but could see no sign of him anywhere. What I needed was a map! Yes, what I needed was the tourist's guide to Grublin City. Yeah, right, like that ever existed. I'd just have to fly low and hope I could spot him – or – I could just use the sixth sense aerial all pilp collectors are blessed with! I found a corner to hide behind, closed my eyes and tried to home in on Albert. Hmmm, my reception needed a little fine tuning. I adjusted my wings until I had a crisp signal. Great! I had him. Now I just needed to actually find him! I waited for a chance to emerge without being noticed and then, keeping well tucked into the houses and shops, flew low towards the signal. I made sure my flying technique was similar to the Grublin style i.e. bumping into things and touching the ground every now and then – which wasn't terribly difficult in my present state of mind. Grublins had never quite mastered the art of flying, mainly due do their rather stubby wings and the fact that all Grublins were naturally quite bulky. But where they failed in flying, they more than succeeded as metal craftsmen, which is probably why Albert had come to the Grublins in the first place. The signal was getting much stronger and I could sense him very close to me now. I turned a corner near what might have been a shoppe but it was hard to tell in the dark. Looking through the window I could just make out a clock though and noticed it was coming up to half past eight. Fred would have expected me half an hour ago. I only wished I could have told him what I was up to so that he could have been here too but this was a task I had to do myself. It was my responsibility.

Around the corner form the shop, I caught my first glimpse of Albert since we'd entered the city. He was hovering over the glass roof of what appeared to be a factory of some kind. Screwing my eyes up, I could just make out the lettering; METAL WORKS. So this was where he was meeting Arty, the conniving little swine. Settling down behind a chimney stack, I watched as the light alias my brother continued to flit around the rooftop anxiously. The minutes passed slowly and nothing much happened when suddenly Albert disappeared round the side of the building. I edged closer around the back of the factory, trying to find a window or opening to see what exactly was going on. I struck lucky, for just at the top of the back wall was an air brick. I squashed my ear against it and listened carefully. Three voices, one was obviously a Grublin, another belonged to Arty Granger but the last one I couldn't quite make out. It had a fairy tone with what sounded like ... bits of Grublin dialect thrown in. There was something vaguely familiar about it but it wasn't Albert's voice. He had yet to arrive. I pushed my ear as close as possible until it actually became painful. The third voice was saying something to the others, I knew this voice I was sure. It was an Incisortonian accent and I'd heard it recently ... in town!

'Justt givee mee the antidote, Arty. I've donee your dirtyy work, noww give itt here.'

'But in just a few hours, you will become a fully fledged Grublin, the first of many.' Arty shook something loudly.

I squidged my eye up to the brick. I could just make out the scrawny figure of Arty Granger. He was shaking a grey bottle in someone's face.

'Whatt do youu mean, Artyy?' said the creature.

'You stupid fairy. Look at yourself! Did you really think it was just about you? Didn't you notice some visual changes in other fairies? Didn't you – listenn whenn theyy spokee?'

There was a gasp from inside. These words made sense to the owner of the gasp – though not to me.

'The greyy bottless! Whatt didd youu doo? Telll mee!'

'Well seeing as you will not be a pilp collector much longer, judging by the length of that third nostril, why not?'

I pushed my nose so hard up to the brick that it hurt like hell but I was desperate to see and hear what was happening. Inside the conversation continued.

'You see, my dear. I made a deal with the sprites. They made me this wonderful potion that turns pilp collectors into – well, into Grublins, very slowly of course. After all, I didn't want to attract the wrong sort of attention ...'

The owner of the gasp, gasped again. 'Haven'tt youu alreadyy donee thatt withh thee lightt?'

'Oh, no. I just needed something to distract other fairies attention away from my real plans. That's where you came in, dear. While everyfairy was panicking about the light, they hardly noticed the population of Pilpsville turning grey, growing an extra nostril and developing a strange accent. No, they were far too distracted, thanks to your dear school friends.'

I swallowed hard. It was all my fault. I'd been following the wrong clues.

'II don'tt believee youu,' came a scream from within, ' II meann, thee spritess wouldd neverr doo aa deall withh aa pilpp collectorr. We'ree naturall enemiess afterr alll.'

'Well, yes – but when I could guarantee them something they so desperately wanted – for life – well, they could hardly refuse, could they?'

Pigging hell, he was going to give them our magic dust.

'You see,' he continued, 'I will shortly own the pilp plant, thanks to your pilp collecting skills – and I will need a willing and obedient workforce. That's where our new Grublins come in. Very soon, there will be no pilp collectors left in this pathetic world to collect pilps so all the pilps will be taken, yes taken, by the newly transformed Grublins. I will then grow rich and powerful as they attend my every whim and will have no need for magic dust at all, which is where the sprites fit in. Do you understand now, my dear Phyllis?'

Phyllis! Phyllis Router the rotten liar! All this time it was her! Flipping hell! It all fell into place now; the red mark, turning grey, her speech, the beady eyes and the long nose. She'd taken the Grublin potion and was slowly turning into one. Phyllis had been *the light* – and all this time I'd thought it was Albert!

Chapter Eighteen

Shocked and alarmed, I flew silently back to the factory rooftop. The weather had taken a turn for the worse and a heavy mist was now forming. As I landed I spotted Albert now lying flat on the rooftop looking through the glass. Reaching far into his pocket, he cautiously pulled out a picture taker. He took several snaps and then as he turned, caught sight of me hovering in the corner.

'Aggie? What are you doing here, of all places?' he whispered.

Guiltily, I looked down at the floor. 'I'm so sorry, Albert. I really thought it was you – I thought you were the light. I followed you here.'

'You thought it was me, how? After all those clues Phyllis kindly left us too. But I did have an idea that you suspected me, what with the way you were trailing me.' He gave me a wink.

'Oh, Albert. What a fool I've been. If you only knew Arty was really up to ...'

'Aggie, I do know. I heard everything. And you haven't been a fool at all, why if you hadn't have taken such an interest and pursued the light so vigorously then we wouldn't all be here now to save the day.'

'We?'

'Well, you didn't think we'd let you take all the

glory did you?' A familiar line followed by two familiar figures. Flitting across the roof came Fred and Bessie.

'When you didn't turn up for our meeting I knew where you'd gone,' he continued, 'so I found Bessie and we followed you.'

'But *how* did you know I'd come here?'

'Why do you think I wanted to meet you, Aggie? I had found out that Phyllis was the light and I wanted to share it with you. Albert had already gone on ahead to try and capture their dealings on film to use as evidence.'

'But I thought Albert was the light. All the evidence pointed to him the pictures, the drawings, the strange disappearances. And you seemed so moody!' I looked at Albert apologetically.

'No more than usual really, huh?' Albert replied, grinning mischievously.

We quickly filled the others in on what Arty had really been up to and his plan to rid the world of tooth fairies. We'd got to the part where he'd have complete control when a loud crash in the far corner of the roof distracted us.

'What the hell's that?' cried Albert.

We scattered to the shadows, hoping to conceal ourselves.

A small hand reached out to pick up the object that had been dropped, a bottle – a *grey* bottle. Three small faces appeared, each carrying a guilty look.

'S-S-Sorryy,' said the red haired one.

'W-W-We justt wanted to helpp,' said the miserable looking one.

'nff uppp.' said the cabbage, examining the floor meekly.

The noise caused the inhabitants of the factory to look up and in an instant the game was up.

'We'd better get out of here quick,' said Albert, picking the bottle up and giving Myrtle and Gilbert a certain look which made them stare immediately at the floor.

'Nott soo quicklyy II thinkk!' came a voice from behind me. As I turned, I was face to face with the three conspirators; Arty Granger, Phyllis Router and presumably Meltiee the metall workerr.

'Lett themm go,' shouted Phyllis. 'They'vee gott no prooff,' she looked directly at Albert '... havee youu?'

'No, no, no, dear Phyllis,' began Arty, 'We can't possibly let them go now, they know far too much.'

Myrtle began to snivel in the corner and there was a puddle where Gilbert was standing.

'Oh not again,' Bessie muttered under her breath. Looking at Gilbert in disbelief, she added, 'It's last Pilpblast all over again!'

Victor continued to examine the floor, not daring to look up.

'So what are you going to do then?' I asked nervously, looking round for an escape route. 'What are you going to do to us?'

'Well, my dear, the metal works are always in need of extra hands to keep the factory ticking over, don't you think, Meltiee?' He looked across to the Grublin who was relentlessly whacking a heavy metal chain onto his hand.

'O, yeahh, Mrr Grangerr, indeedd. Alwayss inn needd off moree workerss.'

He clicked his grubby fingers together and the sky grew dark as a dozen or more ugly long nosed Grublins settled on the factory roof. They drew their weapons – potion filled grey bottles – from behind their backs and shook them sadistically.

'Take them down, take them all including this one,' Arty pushed Phyllis into the awaiting hands of a Grublin. 'She's no more use to us now,' he scoffed nastily.

'Youu can't do thiss, Artyy,' screamed Phyllis. 'You promisedd me creditss to helpp my familyy. That's thee onlyy reasonn I didd it.'

'Oh boo hoo, seems you're not the only liar, huh dear?' He turned to fly away but was soon stopped in his tracks by a sharp blow to the back of his head.

Phyllis's shoe fell to the ground with a shudder. You could almost feel the rage and anger as Arty turned around, his hand clasped to his head.

'Oh, you'll pay for that, sweetie. You mark my words.' He gestured at Meltiee with his free hand.

'Okayy, takee themm down,' he said.

An almighty scuffle broke out as we tried frantically to escape their grubby clutches but there were too many of them. Myrtle and Bessie were captured in an instant and were held under the bulging arms of the nearest Grublin. As much as we tried, there was no escape. They were far too powerful. Then through the falling mist, I saw a gap in their line up and made a dash for it, only to be pulled back violently by my arm which at once dislocated itself from my shoulder. The pain seared through my body leaving me in no position to move any further. One by one they managed to catch us all – well, all except Gilbert! Then even he was quickly backed into a corner but he was not going without a fight.

'Don't youu touch mee or – you'll be sorryy.' Gilbert tried to stand his ground but was quickly surrounded. 'I have a weaponn and I'mm not afraidd to use itt.' He patted his stomach gently.

'Ohh, yeahh likee whatt??'

Hmm, like what?

'Like thiss!' He lifted his top to reveal a small green face with the most enormous green mouth. 'Let 'emm have itt, Victor.'

'epo'u gpshfuu uif fbsqmvhtt!'

'Oh, yeahh.' Gilbert thrust his hand in his trouser pocket and pulled out some tiny blue balls which he threw to each of us in turn.

'Quickk put these inn before he ...' Too late!

'BBBBBBBBBBBBBBBBBBIIIIIIIIIIIIIIIIIIIIIIIIIIIIIIIIII!!!'
which could probably be roughly translated as;
'AAAAAAAAAAAAAAAAAAAAHHHHHHHHHHHH!!!'

I rammed the blue earplugs in my ears as the
Grublin holding me released his fearsome grip and
fell hard to the ground, rolling around, his hands
desperately trying to cover his ears. The rooftop soon
became littered with writhing bodies, clasping their
ears and moaning loudly.

'Makee itt stopp, makee itt stopp.'

'Quickly, we've got to get out of here now. Victor's
only given us a few minutes head start,' shouted
Fred. 'We've got to take advantage of it.'

He flew over to where Phyllis was lying clutching
hard at her ears and handed over some ear plugs.
'Come on, you're coming with us.'

'I-I-I can'tt, nott afterr alll I'vee done.' Her
transformation into a Grublin was almost
complete.

'That's precisely why you must come. You need
to tell everyone what Arty's been up to.'

I yanked her up by the arm, pulling her into the
air. The adrenaline rushing through my body seemed
to mask the pain in my shoulder well, leaving me to
concentrate on the task at hand – escape!

'What about the antidote, Aggie?' shouted Bessie
who was bending over Arty's curled up body.

Reaching inside Arty's jacket she found and pulled out a handful of small glass bottles containing a brown liquid. She threw one to Phyllis who guzzled it down with speed. We could only wait and hope now.

Two miniatures Grublin-fairies held out their hands eagerly for a brown bottle, snatching them greedily before pouring the foul smelling liquid down their throats. Another bottle was rolled to the feet of the screaming sprite.

'Come on, we must fly,' I screamed, as we moved off.

The others followed quickly.

'What aboutt Victor? We can'tt just leave himm here,' cried Gilbert.

'He'll find his own way back, Gilbert. He's given us a chance to escape, let's not waste it.' Bessie grabbed his arm, leaving poor Gilbert reaching out frantically into the air for Victor. As we moved quickly through the night sky towards Pilpsville, his high pitched screams could still be heard lingering in the air. All the time Victor was screaming we would be safe. When his screaming stopped we would really have to worry. That's when the trouble would begin.

Chapter Nineteen

Pilpsville was still some way off and it had been some time since we had last heard Victor's screaming.

'I'm so tiredd,' sobbed Myrtle, trembling, 'and I'm scaredd.' The antidote was kicking in as her voice began to return to normal.

'Just push as hard as you can, Myrtle, we've got to keep going.' I tried to comfort her but truth be told, I was exhausted too.

An eerie gushing noise, growing louder by the minute, now followed our movements. Grublins! They must be on our trail.

'Come on you lot, come on. They're onto us,' shouted Albert, grabbing Myrtle by the hand.

'Come on, move!!' He flapped his wings furiously and sped ahead of us.

Bessie was still struggling with Gilbert who was crying out desperately for Victor and fighting against her every move. Phyllis was still hanging on tightly to me. She hadn't said a word since we'd left Grublin City.

The gushing had grown so loud. They were almost on top of us. I turned in mid-flight and could just make out the bulky forms of the Grublins as they began their descent.

'Pull up, pull up,' screamed Albert. We all followed his lead as he soared upwards. We were still on course for Pilpsville but by now, Myrtle was hysterical and was in sore need of a slap to the face. Gilbert had been told to shut up several times by Bessie who was growing steadily tired of his calling for Victor.

'Down, down,' shouted Albert. But it was no good they were so near I could hear them, shouting and screaming at us.

We were done for. Pilpsville was still ten minutes away and there was no way we could keep going like this.

Suddenly Phyllis pulled on my arm.

'I've gott something ...' she whispered quietly.

'Save it for later, Phyllis. You can tell everyone when we ...'

'I've gott something thatt could helpp, haven't II?' She reached into her rucksack and pulled out a shiny metal object. 'It'ss a fast flying packk or FFP. The Grublins madee it.' It was the two tube thingy in the flesh – or rather in the metal.

'Quickk, help mee into it.' She scrambled into the jacket, calling out to Albert and Bessie at the same time. As they stopped and looked round she pulled a yellow cord on the jacket and the bottom of the tubes fell to the sides.

'Hang onto my armm, Aggie. Everyone else linkk arms but don't stop flapping. It'll givee us an extra boost. We mightt just make it ...'

'Oh no you don't, dearie,' came a shout from

above. Arty, naturally quicker than the Grublins, had finally caught up with us. 'You're going nowhere.' He reached out to grab Phyllis by the leg.

'Now that's where you're wrong, Arty,' she shouted, sounding and looking a whole lot better. She tugged at a red cord and flames shot out of the two tubes, propelling us all upwards, leaving Arty screeching and shaking his fist far below.

The Grublins were still coming but thanks to the FFP we would be in Pilpsville before they could catch up with us.

As the minutes went by I began to feel more at ease although my arm was aching terribly where Phyllis was hanging on to it.

'Not long now,' called Albert.

I could just make out the border of Pilpsville a little way ahead. My relief at the thought of home was short lived as the pain in my shoulder resurfaced, causing me to jerk wildly.

'Aggie, what have you done ...' To my horror, I'd unwittingly broken the link, causing all and sundry to fall heavily groundwards.

'Don't worry, you keep going,' called Phyllis. 'I'll dive down and get them.'

With that she pulled a blue cord on the FFP and was gone, groundwards.

The Grublins were now far enough in the distance but my stupid error had lost us time. I had to get to the pilp plant and raise the alarm. I flew over the borders, back through Great Molaring, which was strangely deserted, and into the communal centre. It was a sight for sore arms. The whole area was packed full of fairies from all over Pilpsville, clutching brooms, mops and other strange weapons. I could see Ma and Pa in front of the pilp plant with a worried looking Mrs Router. Next to them was Mr Fettock who seemed to have a firm hold on Mr Cruet.

'Come on, Aggie. Where are the others?' shouted Fettock. 'Why aren't they with you?' Oh, marvellous – it would all be my fault again.

'We know what's been going on, Aggie. We've been waiting for you all to bring the culprits back,' Fettock continued as I landed next to Ma.

'How do you know?'

'Fred and Albert – they followed your leads and asked me to get everyone ready to receive *visitors*!'

It was only a matter of minutes until they arrived. Phyllis had just managed to keep enough distance between the Grublins and herself. I flew up and grabbed hold of Albert who was still hanging on for dear life at the back.

'Just hold on Albert.' We swept down and down, landing safely in front of the pilp plant.

'Hooray!' A cheer went up from the awaiting crowd.

I blushed deeply, embarrassed by the sudden fame we'd found.

'Save your cheers for later,' said Fettock, pointing to the sky which was rapidly growing darker. 'Grab your weapons – quickly. The *visitors* are about to arrive.'

The rancid smell of Grublin filled the night air, almost suffocating the assembled fairy mob. As they flew nearer, their hideous features shone out clearly, frightening the last adventurous fairylets back into their homes.

'Here, take this. You're going to need it.' A large wooden mop was thrust into my hand by Mrs Flinge. She smiled sweetly at me before handing out other weapons to Bessie and Albert.

I was exhausted but prepared to fight, even if it was with only one good arm.

'Let's get you three inside until the *visitors* have been *welcomed*,' said Ma, herding Myrtle, Gilbert and Phyllis gently into the reception area of the plant. 'Just sit down and get your breath back. You've had more than your share of fighting for one night.'

They didn't argue. They were too badly shaken by the whole experience.

'Come on, Ma,' called Pa anxiously. 'They're here!'

And here they most certainly were. Down they crashed one after the other, landing noisily and clumsily in any available space. Eyes gawping, nostrils flaring, mouths open.

'What are we waiting for?' screamed Fred, tucking

his broomstick under his arm, 'Let 'em have it – AAAARRRRGGGHHH!'

Bodies flew in all directions, crashing into buildings, falling to the floor. It was terrifying. Grunts and groans filled the air as broomsticks and mop handles collided with Grublin body parts. Squeals and shrieks filled the air as fists and heads collided with fairy body parts. It was a bloody battle with neither side prepared at this stage to submit. Having just the one good arm, I decided to wait for my moment before pitching in and hid under a nearby porch while the battle continued. A loud screech made me look to the far end of the pilp plant where pairs of Grublins had singled out lone fairies and pinned them to the wall with their grubby hands. They were pulling at their captive's wings, tearing through the fine webs that covered them rendering them useless.

'Fred,' I shouted, 'come here. I need to get over there.' I pointed to the wall where another fairy was screaming out in pain.

'I'm a bit busy at the moment, Aggie!' He was just finishing off a rather small Grublin with a garden rake. 'Get Bessie to help. Oh great, see what you've done now!' The small Grublin, seeing Fred in conversation, had fled, – half jumping, half flying – into the night sky.

'I can't find her,' I shouted above the din, 'You know what she's like with Grublins.'

She was probably hiding somewhere, waiting for the Grublins to be beaten.

I scanned the crowd frantically for any sign of her. Then as I turned back to the porch a loud piercing scream hit me hard.

'AGGIE! Grublins, Aggie. Help me!'

It was Bessie! Two grotesque Grublins had picked her up and were flying her towards the end of the pilp plant.

'AGGIE, PLEASE!' she cried loudly, tears flowing down her frightened face. 'PLEASE!!'

'I'm coming Bess, I'm coming.'

I mustered what strength I had left and pushed upwards away from the porch. My wings were tight and my arm ached dreadfully. I could feel the beginnings of cramp starting to set in so chose to hover just above the battle scene. Grabbing Grublin hands shot into the air as I flew past but they were quickly pulled back by battling fairies. I still had the mop Mrs Flinge had given me and swung it wildly whenever a Grublin head appeared.

'AGGIE, QUICKLY,' Bessie screamed above the crowd. She was pinned against a wall by the two Grublins who were taking it in turns to pick at her wings. I grabbed a broom handle from a passing fairy and made my landing.

'Hey, you,' I said, tapping the larger Grublin of the two on the shoulder with the mop.

'Whatt ...'

Crash! I bought the head of the mop straight down on the back of his neck. He collapsed instantly in a dirty heap on the floor.

'Quick, Bess, grab this.' I threw the broom handle to her and we set about dealing with the other one.

'Ouchh, ouchh, sorryy, sorryy, pleasee lett mee goo.' The smaller Grublin crouched on the floor holding its arms over its head as Bessie and me delivered broom and mop blows.

'II won'tt doo itt againn, promisee. Havee pityy.' He crawled towards Bessie's leg and pawed at her knee.

'After what you've done? Get off her.' I lifted my mop ready to give him another clout when Bessie suddenly stepped in.

'Oh, just get out of here, you disgusting creature!' She stood aside as the Grublin brought itself up to it's full height. It spread its scrawny wings and was preparing to take off as she tugged at its ear.

'You owe me one, Grublin and one day I'll call the favour in. Now get your smelly face out of mine.' She gave him a hefty kick sending him on his way home to Grublin City.

'Pigging hell, Bess. What was that all about?' I said, pulling her around to face me.

'Dunno, Aggie. It just didn't seem that scary any more. It was just little, smelly and pathetic.'

I suppose she was right. Mind you, that theory was shot out of the window as soon as we headed back to the main battle.

'Ahhh, Grublins!' screamed Bessie. Grublin phobia had quickly set back in.

But we were not going to play any further part in the battle.

'Over here, you two,' Ma shouted and beckoned us to the pilpminder's doorway. 'Join the others.'

Huddled in a corner were Phyllis, Myrtle and Gilbert.

Fred followed a few minutes later.

As battle of the broom handle was coming to an end, Ma wanted us out of the way for the final flurry. We sat down, not daring to look at each other or speak, but answers were still needed.

It was Phyllis, of all fairies, who started the conversation. 'How did you know it was me, Albert?'

'Well, for a start you told Fred and Aggie different stories about the light and why would you need to do that?'

'But she *always* lies, Albert – no offence meant Phyllis,' I said, clutching my arm, the pain now returning with vigour.

'None taken,' she replied sadly.

'But there were other factors,' said Fred. 'The attacks only took place when Phyllis was on the nightsgritch.'

'Yeah, and the other night in the juice bar I spotted you and Arty arguing in the corner.' I threw in my evidence on behalf of the prosecution.

'And turning grey and growing a three nostrilled nose may have also given the game away! Just a little obvious, don't you think?' said Albert.

'Yeah, it all makes sense now, but why on earth did you think it was Albert, Aggie?' asked Fred.

'It was those pictures that really did it. I think I had all these things buzzing around my head like the lack of pilps collected, extra sacks appearing.'

' ... the piece of paper you took from under my mattress!' said Fred.

' ... and the piece of paper I took from under your mattress, Fred. So I had convinced myself that it was Albert. When I looked at the pictures in the library I saw what I thought was Albert and that was it. Then all I needed to do was follow him to find out if I was right.'

'But you never said anything, you never told anyfairy of your ideas,' said Fred.

'Well, I had to be sure,' I said, 'and after all, he's my brother.'

Cries of 'Yuk, pass me a bucket, I'm going to be sick,' came from the corner where Gilbert was still snivelling.

Phyllis began to sob heavily. The guilt was obviously beginning to trickle in to her brain thick and fast now.

The battle outside seemed to have come to an end. Fred popped his head out of the door to see what was happening.

'Well, come on, tell us. Is it over? Can we go?' sobbed Gilbert, wiping his dripping nose on his sleeve.

'It looks like all the Grublins have been sent packing and Arty Granger is being sat on by Aggie's mum and Mrs Router. Oh, hang on, Mr Fettock's coming this way.' He retreated back inside quickly as Mr Fettock opened the door widely.

'Out you come, now. We're just waiting for Ferret to arrive to deal with Arty. The Grublins have returned home battle scarred ...'

Broom handle scarred more like!

' ... and will hopefully think twice next time,' he concluded.

'But Mr Fettock, I don't understand. You said the light was an angry firefly. You said there was nothing to worry about ...' I said, recalling our earlier conversation at school.

'I didn't have all the facts then. I knew that if I told you that, you'd have to find the out the truth – being the busy body you are!' He gave a sort of smile-smirk as he finished.

'But you could have helped us. We could have been turned into Grublins!'

'I'd have slowed you down. I just asked Fred to keep me informed of your progress.'

I could see his point. He wasn't exactly built for the kind of escapades we'd been up to. He ushered us outside.

Pa was waiting for us, as was Fred's mum. He made his way over to me and taking the scarf off from around his neck, made a sling for my shoulder to rest in.

'There, that'll serve you 'til we get home.' He smiled proudly at me.

Phyllis stared at her mum who returned her gaze but then gave her a small smile as a comfort. Phyllis sobbed again.

It wasn't long before Ferret arrived.

'So what have you been up to now, Arthur?'

'Perhaps you'd better ask Aggie,' said Mr Fettock. 'She's been in it from the start!'

A large crowd began to gather around me as the story, which started with a mysterious light, unfolded in front of them. They listened in astonishment to how Arty conned Phyllis into collecting enough pilps for him, using the FFP, to buy the pilp plant from Mr Cruet. Dumbfounded, they heard how he made a deal to exchange magic dust for a potion, with our sworn enemies, – the sprites. But the worst was to come and I could almost see the anger surge within them when they learnt of the fate Arty had in store for them all – his fairies into Grublins trick! And how he planned to use them as slave labour to at the pilp plant, achieving his aim to be the most powerful pilp collector in all of Pilpsville – indeed the only pilp collector!

The crowd, now an angry mob, turned quickly from me to face Arty who was being restrained by Mr Fettock and Ferrett. Surprisingly, he still stood tall, glaring straight through the centre of the crowd – at me.

'What are we going to do with him?' somefairy shouted.

Mr Fettock shrugged his shoulders – then looked at me.

'What do you think, Aggie?'

I turned and caught sight of Fred and Bessie. They nodded in agreement knowing exactly what punishment I was thinking of.

'How about a taste of his own medicine?' I threw him the grey bottle that I'd found on the Grublin factory roof. As he caught it he nodded and yanked Arty's head back. 'Look what the kind fairy has given you, don't forget to say thank you.'

Arty opened his mouth to speak and it didn't look like the words 'thank you' were the ones forming in his mouth. Just as he did, Ferret poured some of the grey liquid down his throat making Arty cough furiously.

'You ungrateful wretch, drink it down properly.'

I swung a shiny brown bottle playfully by my side whilst glaring straight into Arty's eyes, which were now slowly started to bulge. His skin began to pale as drop by drop the potion began to kick in.

'What will you do with him now?' I asked.

'I think a spell in Mursham Marshes is most definitely on the agenda, don't you? said Mr Fettock, tightening his grip on Arty's arm.

There were gasps from the crowd. No fairy had been sent to Mursham Marshes in almost fifty years. The island, surrounded by treacherous and foul smelling marshes, was the worst punishment Pilpsville could offer. Arty would have to be flown there and then, once landed, his wings would be clipped so as he could not escape. It was a cruel punishment for a cruel crime.

Arty was marched through the angry crowd, his fairy features diminishing rapidly as the Grublin inside took over. His angry gaze fell onto the brown bottle I had at my side as he was jostled into the path of where I stood. If looks could kill ...

'Ohh youu think you'ree so cleverr, don'tt youu deariee! Butt I'lll bee outt one day soonn andd then I'lll ...'

He was pulled away quickly by Ferrett before he could finish but I understood the threat.

'Take no notice, Aggie. He's just angry that he was caught.' Bessie patted my back as if to console me.

'Yeah, he's just all mouth. A few months in the marshes will sort him out,' said Fred.

'You're right, Fred. He's got what he deserved,' I said, giving off an air of calm. But deep down inside I knew that when he did get out he would be desperately seeking revenge – on me!

But Arty wasn't the only one at fault. Mr Cruet had a question or two to answer.

'Did you really think we'd let you sell up?' Pa asked.

Wilfred Cruet eyed the ground nervously. 'Thanks to these fairychids, we knew about the one hundred year contract and its thirty day clause anyway. One way or another you'd have been stopped and thankfully you were,' Pa said, glancing over to Mr Fettock.

'Yes, as soon as Aggie discovered the light we began to start piecing bits together. We didn't have to do too much though as they did all the hard work for us.'

So that must be worth a very large reward or at least a medal ...

'Well done!' Hmm, not quite what I had in mind.

Back on the ground there was still the small matter of Phyllis's involvement.

She looked so sad, so embarrassed by it all.

'You could have cost us our livelihood, Phyllis, do you realise that?' said Mrs Router, trying to understand her actions.

'It might be best if you take her home. I think she's been as much a victim as we have,' said Mr Fettock.

'Yes, perhaps you're right. Come on, Phyllis, let's talk about this later.' Mrs Router took hold of poor Phyllis's hand and they too headed home.

'Well, Aggie, all's well that ends well, so to speak,' said Fred, 'I-I'll see you tomorrow night then,' he added expectantly.

'Tomorrow night?'

'The pilpblast – tomorrow!' He looked at me as if I were mad.

'Ah, yes, the pilpblast. Oh, sorry Fred. I'm not …'

'Take no notice, Fred. She'll be there …' Myrtle looked at me sternly. My little sister was pulling rank on me! Little madam!

'Come along, Fred – and bring the snivelling wreck with you,' shouted Fred's mum.

'Right,' said Ma, 'let's get you lot home. A good night's rest is what you need after all this excitement. We'll drop Bessie off on the way.'

'What about Pa?' I asked.

'Well, he and Mr Fettock need to have a little talk with Mr Cruet about amending his contract. I think we'll see a few changes there.'

'So the pilp plant won't be sold.'

'Oh, no, not now. Thanks to you and your friends, the one hundred year clause has relapsed as the thirty days are up just about … now!'

The clock on the pilp plant struck midnight.

'Come on, let's get home.' She pulled me up gently by the hand. Myrtle swept underneath to support my throbbing shoulder.

'Hurry up, Bess. Grab hold of Ma.'

'No, it's okay,' called Albert. 'She can fly with me,' he took Bessie's hand as she passed and she grinned broadly at him.

Oh yuk, not again! Although that meant that *she* was no longer keen on Fred ...

Below us the scene of broom handle carnage disappeared from view as we headed, at last, for home.

Chapter Twenty

We all slept in late the next morning which was hardly surprising given the previous night's events and due to the sleeping potion Ma had given me. It was only the sound of humming outside the window that eventually woke me. Not being a morning fairy, I was none too pleased.

'Who's making that blinking noise? Fairies trying to sleep in here.'

I threw back the curtains angrily, forgetting the poor condition my shoulder was in. Youch!!

'Blimey Aggie!' Myrtle mumbled, pulling the covers over her face.

'Bessie? What the hell are you doing here so early? Go away, we're shattered.'

But she was oblivious to my grumbling.

'Do you think Albert prefers blue or red?' she grinned and twiddled her hair round her finger. 'How would I ...'

'How would you what?' I said impatiently.

She carried on regardless, '... only I'm not sure which dress to wear tonight.'

Then she started to hum again!

'ALBERT! Bessie wants to ask you something,' I shouted down the hallway.

When I returned to the window her face was a picture. Even Myrtle got up to have a look.

'You're so mean, Aggie,' she giggled.

'Yep, and don't you forget it.'

'Are you really not coming tonight?' she asked.

'Yeah, I'd rather stay in. So many fairies still think I let the sprites in that I'd only feel uncomfortable. Don't go saying anything to Ma and Pa. I don't want to spoil their night ... besides I've nothing to wear anyway and my shoulder's sore.' I rubbed it for good measure.

'But Fred's expecting you to be there,'

Hmmm, Fred.

'No, Myrtle, I've made my decision and that's that. You go. Gilbert's desperate to dance with you.' She blushed as I spoke.

'It won't be the same though if you don't come.'

'Thanks, Myrtle but I'm staying put. Now you'd better get to the door quickly if you want to overhear what those two are saying!' I knew how she loved to eavesdrop and that would provide me with an escape route from her questions.

Ma had also been rudely awakened by Bessie in 'lurve' mode and was pottering around noisily in the kitchen. This was my chance to talk to her. I had one or two, well let's face it, a bucketful of lies to get off my chest!

I explained the lies ... and why I lied ... and how I would never do it again – the guilt would kill me. Her reaction was somewhat indifferent. I'd expected something but not this. Then she dropped a bomb.

'I know you lied.'

She knew I'd lied? Damn dragonflies. Hate Dragonflies.

'But how ...'

'I'm the mum. I'm supposed to know, it's my job. And your brother and sister were great assistants!'

Nice dragonflies. Damn Bugface. Hate Bugface. Damn Albert. Hate Albert.

'Yes, they explained everything, each and every lie you told, to me in great detail.' She looked at me disappointedly. 'But,' she continued, 'when I found out the reasons behind the lies I could sort of understand.'

Nice Bugface. Nice Albert.

'That doesn't mean you can do it again, right? Lies always catch up with you. They wait round the corner and pounce when you're not looking. The more you tell the bigger the hole gets ...' She looked around the room for inspiration while I sank deeper and deeper into the guilt pit.

'... oh what a tangled web we spin when those little lies fall in ...'

'I think she's got the message Ma,' Pa came to my rescue and poured himself a smint tea.

And a big hug from Ma told me I was forgiven and a lesson had been learnt!

****

Afternoon quickly followed what was left of the morning and before I knew it early evening had arrived. The house was bustling with excitement as the rest of the family made themselves ready for the pilpblast. Ma and Pa had already been down to the community hall to help with the final decorations and I had it on good authority – Myrtle – that the band were 'really cool'.

I'd settled myself down for a little rest after Ma insisted on me taking a draught of firl to relieve the shoulder pain. No sooner had I closed my eyes when the sound of somefairy creeping around startled me. It was Myrtle. She sat on the edge of her bed swinging her legs anxiously.

'Are you sure you won't come, Aggie? Are you really, really sure?' she looked at me strangely and grinned. 'Only you know how I said I wouldn't ...'

'Oh, Myrtle, you haven't told Ma have you ...'

'No, stop! You're doing it again. I haven't said anything but I have done something.' The strange grin appeared again.

'You haven't set another web trap have you, only I'll get the blame for ...'

'No, who cares about Gertie Cruet? No, I've done something much better than that. Now close your eyes.'

'Myrtle, if you're going to put ice down my back again ...'

'Just close your eyes, Aggie,' said Ma softly, stepping into the room.

As asked, I closed my eyes tightly not knowing what to expect.

'Now hold out your arms, I mean arm!,' said Myrtle.

I held out my arm and felt something light and soft lying on it.

'Open them – open your eyes, look!' She was jumping up and down.

Across my arm lay the most beautiful red dress I'd ever seen. It was even better than the purple dress. It was perfect. It was unique.

'W-What? H-How? W-When?'

'I made it for you, for you to wear tonight at the pilpblast,' said Myrtle. 'Ma helped me.'

'But I said ...'

'Just try it on, Aggie, then decide,' said Ma. 'It'll go nicely with your red boots,' she added as she left the room again.

My little sister was certainly full of surprises. Never under estimate the powers of sisterhood!

I stood in front of the mirror. It was certainly a beautiful dress and it fitted perfectly but Gertie Cruet would still be there acting the heroine, and I'd still be 'the one who let the sprites in'.

'What's the matter, don't you like it?' Myrtle asked.

'Oh, I love it, it's just ...'

'I told you not to think about Gertie Cruet ...'

There was a knock on the bedroom door. It was Pa.

'Come on you two, we'll be late ...'

'But Pa ...' I pleaded.

'No buts, let's go!' He gestured us towards the door. I was going to the pilpblast, like it or not!

****

The music drifted down the street to greet us. We flew to the hall as a family passing many other fairies dressed up in their finery.

The hall was quite full when we arrived but there was no sign of Fred and his family. Bessie was already there with her parents. She had chosen to wear blue which was handy for me. Albert noticed her immediately and made his way over to talk to her. Ma and Pa decided to embarrass Myrtle and me by doing the fly dance in the middle of the floor.

'Could they be more obvious?' I said to Myrtle. She started to giggle then stopped and nudged me.

'Look, Gertie Cruet's arrived.' Oh and couldn't you tell! Once again the flies swarmed around the jam pot – so to speak. A purple jam pot – she had my dress on.

'Take no notice. What we did yesterday was much bigger and besides, we all know it wasn't her who saved the day,' said a friendly voice in my ear. It was

Fred. 'Wow, that's some dress, Aggie.'

I felt myself blush.

'I made it, I made it,' Myrtle did her jumping up and down like a demented grasshopper trick.

'Where's the rest of you?' I asked, trying to calm down my blushes.

'Well, mum and dad have gone over to the bar to get a drink.'

'So your dad's back then?' I turned my head slightly, hoping the redness had gone.

'Yeah, he's been working on new uses for the magic dust.'

A sharp prod in the back made me jump suddenly.

'Where's Gilbert?' Myrtle interrupted rudely, looking round the hall.

'Blimey, Myrtle,' I said. ' Whatever happened to excuse me?'

'Okay, okay, *excuse me*. Now where's Gilbert?'

'I was just about to say! He said he had to do something first, then he'll make an appearance,' Fred replied. 'He's still upset about losing Victor,' he added.

Poor Gilbert, you couldn't help but feel sorry for him.

'Well, while we're waiting for him, shall we get ourselves a juice? Mrs Cheric's invented some new ones especially for tonight,' Myrtle said, satisfied that Gilbert would show later.

Moving across the room I exchanged glances with Phyllis Router who was only there because her mum had insisted that she came and faced up to the mistakes she'd made. She sat awkwardly at the table with the other little Routers, sipping her juice nervously. The antidote had worked and her face was almost entirely back to normal. It was only the third nostril that gave any indication that she was ever a Grublin. Across the hall, Gertie Cruet and her cronies pointed and mouthed the word 'loser' at her and sniggered loudly. Oh, if only I could wipe that smirk off her ugly face.

Phew! What was that? What a pong! What a stink! What a stench!

Through the open window, a yellowy wisp floated gently upwards and across the hall. It fell sharply to the floor, weaving in and out of the many ankles that tried to step over it. Gathering speed, it completely circled the room before coming to a dramatic halt just above Gertie Cruet's head. Silence filled the room as all eyes were fixed upon it ... and of course the unknowing victim below it.

'What? What you all looking at, huh?' she spun around on the spot, glaring madly at the crowd which was slowly retreating backwards to the edges of the hall.

Oh dear, now what's that old saying? Ah yeah, what goes up must come ... down!

So that's where he'd been! He said he'd get her

back – and her legs and her neck and her arms …

'Help, Daddy, help. I'm being stinked at. Daddy, where are you, DADDY! Aaaahhhh.' She ran around the room trying to shake him off but he was going nowhere.

'Help me,' she screamed, pulling at her dress, shaking her head frantically.

Fred stepped forward with a jar.

'Aaaaaarrrrggghhh.'

'Perhaps you'd like to tell everyone the truth, Gertie. The truth about how the sprites were driven out,' he said calmly, tapping the lid of the jar.

'Aaaaarrrggghhh, just get him off me,' she yelled.

'Gilbert, hover!' ordered Fred, and Gilbert the smell hovered – just above her head.

'Okay, okay, it wasn't me who got rid of the sprites, I just let him out, okay!' she spat angrily.

'Well, no it's not okay. Tell the good fairies who it was, say his name nice and loud.'

'Gilbert,' she mumbled under her breath, eyes to the floor.

'I'm sorry, but I don't think we heard you.'

'GILBERT!! Okay, happy now? It was Gilbert who got rid of the sprites not me.' She stamped her foot crossly and escaped across the crowded room to where her father sat waiting.

The smell stopped hovering and swept upwards to the ceiling before disappearing swiftly out of the main door. In a matter of seconds Gilbert had re-entered the hall in his fairy form.

'Three cheers for Gilbert,' came a cry and Gilbert was hoisted onto fairy shoulders and held aloft for all to see.

'Oh I'm so proud of him,' bawled Fred's mum.

'How'd you do that?' I asked, trying not to look up his nose.

'I did a deal with Old Skifle,' he shouted, 'in return for another ten minutes of smell.'

Just what the deal was he wouldn't say.

I left Gilbert high in his element and headed for a seat near the cake table. Myrtle was quick on my heels and plonked herself down heavily in the seat opposite.

'If only Victor was here, it'd make everything perfect,' Myrtle sighed sadly. 'He could be a fully fledged Grublin by now, poor thing.'

'Sacrifices have to be made sometimes,' I said.

'But he's probably been put to work at the Metal Works ...' More sighing!

'Try not to think about it and while you're at it, try not to keep kicking my ankles!'

'I didn't do anything.' Myrtle pulled her legs to the side on the table. 'See, I haven't even got my shoes on.'

'Ouch! Well something's having a go at my foot big time.'

Myrtle fished about under the table then

disappeared beneath the great white, cake covered cloth.

Her head popped up. She grinned widely. 'I think I've found the problem.'

A small green face emerged slowly, holding tightly onto the edge of the tablecloth.

'Victor! You're okay ... you're not a Grublin!' I said and leant forward to pick him up. He stepped back, still clutching the table cloth, causing the entire cake self-selection buffet to fall crashing to the floor.

'AAARRRGGGHHH! SPRITE!' screamed the fairies.

'bbbssshhhiii! gbjsjft!' screamed the sprite.

'It's okay, he's with me,' shouted Gilbert, climbing down and running across the hall. He swept Victor up in his arms.

'I'm sorry Gilbert, I tried to get to him but he backed away – again,' I explained.

'epo'u xbou up hp up uif cbe gbjsz!' said the sprite sulkily.

'Right, you keep saying that, now tell me why she's a bad fairy!' said Gilbert.

From among the inquisitive watchers who had surrounded Gilbert and Victor, came a wry comment, 'she let them all in, that's why!'

A few heads nodded in agreement.

'Hang on, let the sprite tell us himself.' The portly figure of Mr Fettock stepped forward. 'I understand spritespiel a little and so should be able to confirm what he says.'

Victor began to talk, Gilbert translated and Mr Fettock listened. I just stood still, waiting to hear what I'd done wrong.

Fred sidled up next to me. 'Don't worry, it's probably nothing.'

Victor, through Gilbert, told how the sprites had been searching for the entrance to Pilpsville for three days as they'd run out of magic dust. They hid for ages, listening carefully for any noise that might point them in the right direction. Then they heard loud laughing and sniggering and, following carefully, they spotted three tooth fairies; Gertie, Violet and Petunia! That was it. They knew the entrance was near. They swarmed towards our exit, screeching loudly to frighten and cause panic. They'd spotted the net and had become angry that we would have the cheek to try and stop them. Then the bad fairy – me! – spread herself against the door and wouldn't let them pass – bad fairy! Even when they shouted at her she still wouldn't let them pass – bad fairy! It was only when she was distracted by her friend that they were able to get through.

Mr Cruet, at this point, could be seen scurrying across the back of the hall, horrid daughter in tow.

'So Aggie didn't let the sprites in, on the contrary, she tried to keep them out! What do you say to that, Wilfred?'

Mr Cruet nudged Gertie hastily towards the door. She looked back, her eyes scanning the room looking for something ... or somefairy – me. She gave me the filthiest look ever and something told me that our feud was far from over. I decided to hit back with my deadliest weapon – a manic smile with full set of teeth showing which seemed to do the trick.

'Wilfred!' called Mr Fettock once more.

But he was gone. Apologies didn't come easy to that family. But hey, what did I care? I was in the clear.

Mr Fettock stormed out after the Cruets and very quickly the party atmosphere returned.

'Play something lively now,' Ma shouted to the band. 'Let's make this a pilpblast to remember.'

'As long as it's not the fly dance,' I whispered to Myrtle.

She giggled loudly and nodded.

'At least Gertie Cruet can't spoil the rest of the evening,' I said, relaxing back into my chair.

'No, although she may not enjoy the rest of *her* evening ...' Myrtle's eyes twinkled brightly and a huge grin took over her face.

'Oh heck, what have you done *now*?' I smiled, half knowing what the answer was going to be.

'Nothing much ... but did you notice her face, Aggie? She was looking kind of grey ...'

P.S. To translate from Spritespiel;

Just take the previous letter

in the alphabet!